THE STUFFED MEN
THE COMPLETE CASES OF JIGGER
MASTERS, VOLUME 3

THE STUFFED MEN
THE COMPLETE CASES OF
JIGGER MASTERS, VOLUME 3

ANTHONY M. RUD

POPULAR PUBLICATIONS · 2023

TABLE OF CONTENTS

THE STUFFED MEN

*It Was a Baffling Trail That Jigger
Masters Followed—Priceless Ming Vases
Shattered to Bits and Three Bulging
Corpses Stuffed with the Yellow Death*

1

THE MYSTERY OF THE BURIAL URNS

IN THE DARK room there was an occasional jerky snore. The man in bed turned over, muttered, and threw aside the single blanket covering. The night was warm, even with a steady breeze.

Between the two windows facing north toward Long Island Sound, a red alarm light stuttered on and off—and on again.

"Uh—the hell!" breathed Ralph Marriott, and sat up in bed. "Burglars!"

Chunky, self-willed, inclined to rashness, Marriott slid his bare feet to the floor. He reached one hand down to a leather holster depending from the box spring of his bed. He gripped a .45 Colt automatic.

The red alarm light flickered once more, then went out.

Marriott tiptoed silently over to a phone table, and lifted the receiver.

"Mineola police department," he said softly to the operator. "Yes, police! Dammit girl, I've got *burglars* in the house! Give me the cops." His voice rose to a repressed growl, and he kept his eyes frowning upon the doorway to the upper hall.

A moment later he got the connection. Then he told the facts as he knew them briefly and clearly.

"Ralph Marriott speaking. Pryde Estates, Biskra Bay. Number Ten Shore Road. My alarm shows that there are burglars downstairs. Yes, yes. Of course there are valuable things, but what the hell does that matter? Are you coming? All right. Hurry it up!"

He replaced the receiver. Pistol in hand he tiptoed to the doorway giving upon the upper hall. There were three dim night lamps burning. Ten minutes of two in the morning. Marriott's sixty-year-old spinster sister, and his wife, both slept. The four servants slept on the floor above. Dead stillness.

Yet behind Marriott the red light flickered again. That meant intruders down to business in the east wing, where his almost priceless collections were kept.

Setting his obtuse jaw, and gripping the automatic, Marriott started down the broad staircase. He crouched so his bald head, wisped around with gray, barely showed above the banister.

In his anger and contempt for thieves, Marriott did not

"Go back, you," squealed the Oriental. "Quick—or you die!"

One of the Chinese got in the car to start the motor.

give himself a chance. As he reached the end of the staircase in the lower hall, two indistinguishable figures rose from the blackness at either side, and fell upon him with the silent swiftness of practiced manhandlers.

Some kind of a cloth bag smelling musty and fetid, was jammed over his head and shoulders, muffling his grunt and sudden shout. The shout ended in a choking cough.

The assailants pinned his heavy arms. They wrested away the automatic, though not before it barked once. The bullet ricocheted on the waxed floor of the hall, and buried itself in the baseboard.

Squirming, trying to struggle, Marriott was thrown to the floor. In forty seconds they had him trussed with thin, light rope that cut deep into his fleshy ankles. Silk rope so strong it would have cut off an elephant's leg, before it snapped.

They left him lying there, helpless and furious, breathing with utmost difficulty. Upstairs there was a feminine cry, questioning, a little apprehensive. Then the respectful voice of a male servant. On the second and third floors no one was sure as yet that the noise had really been a shot, or that there was genuine cause for alarm. But they would learn quickly enough.

One of the vague figures padded back past the shapeless, recumbent form of Marriott. The intruder unreeled something that slapped thinly on the floor. He disappeared out the window they had jimmied open, still unreeling.

Another vague form joined him. Then a third. There was silence for half a minute, save for stirrings upstairs, and the muffled sounds of stertorous breathing from the bound man.

Then a sputtering light appeared, climbing through the open window! It came fast. It was "instantaneous" fuse. When lighted, this fuse is consumed at the rate of a foot a second. It is almost impossible to put out, except by chopping through the strand well in advance of the speeding sputter.

It zizzed along the floor, across a rug, leaving a branded welt below its white-hot ash. On into the first of the three galleries where Marriott kept his treasures of silver, hand-worked gold, and fragile porcelain. Into the ceramics gallery, where Marriott only four days before had brought his newest and greatest treasure, a shelf of Ming porcelains so terrifically valuable any two of the larger specimens would have built even this miniature mansion of a house.

On and on, toward that very cabinet and shelf....

Whamm!

It was only a small charge of dynamite, but its effect in that enclosed space filled with delicate things, was appalling. First, it flung away the two davenports placed for tamping, as though they had been wisps of excelsior. Then it tore the Ming cabinet and the wall behind it, filling the air with dust and infinitesimal fragments. It jarred out plate glass from the other cabinets, dropping whole shelves of art objects to the floor.

And the breath of explosion, sucking from the adjacent room, rolled the trussed owner of the collection over and over toward the smoke-filled gallery. Marriott, however, was more than half-suffocated now. He did not know. Vaguely he supposed that an earthquake must be occurring.

THERE HIS WIFE and sister found him. Assisted by the butler and chauffeur, and impeded by the burly Irish cook who ran about uttering squeaky falsetto shrieks like a mad woman, they loosed Marriott's bonds. Then they spooned two gills of Hennessey's Three Star brandy into him. Marriott wheezed and choked his way to full consciousness. By the time the two squad cars full of police arrived, the house owner was sitting up in an armchair. He was pale and shaky, but able to curse the police for their slowness.

Lieutenant Connor, a white-haired, pink-cheeked man in his middle fifties, ignored Marriott's irascibility. With two subordinates Connor searched the gallery. As far as he could see there was no clue whatever, except the burned welt across the floor and rug, up to the window and over the sill.

"Beside the damage, was there anything at all stolen, Mr. Marriott?" Connor asked, mystified at what seemed an act of vandalism without rhyme or reason behind it, "I can see that a lot of that bric-à-brac probably is worth quite a lot of money."

"Bric-à-brac!" gasped Marriott, color flooding back into his cheeks. "Bric—oh, my God! Look here, Lieutenant," he breathed in a sort of resigned helplessness. "The contents of that one cabinet cost me *over three hundred thousand dollars!* The total damage in that one room will run to fully twice that sum. And I want you to get the jealous devil who did it. *Get* him, d'you understand?"

He half-rose, shaking one clenched fist.

Instantly, though, he sank back, breathing short and fast. His blue eyes became glassy. "Some more—brandy!" he gasped thickly. "Send for Doc Andrews, will you, Beale? I—feel like—a stroke was coming!"

While the butler hastened to phone the medico, Mrs. Marriott held a glass of the diluted brandy to her husband's lips. He gulped it down, and again seemed to stave off a stroke or faint.

When seven o'clock arrived, the police had searched the house and grounds thoroughly, finding nothing at all. It was hard to say that there had been no theft at all; but if appearances were truthful, some band of vandals had jimmied a window, picked the lock of the gallery, and there

set a charge of dynamite intended to destroy the most valuable part of Ralph Marriott's collection.

All of the precious Ming porcelain had been reduced
to dust and tiny fragments. Three large burial urns, for
instance, had disappeared. Each of these had cost Ralph
Marriott fifty-thousand dollars, less than one week before
the explosion.

"THE ONLY THING I can say, Mr. Marriott," said Connor,
with a regretful shake of his head, "is that for your sake I am
glad you had them insured. With no more than a private
suspicion against this other collector you think may have
been jealous of you, the law can do nothing. I suggest you
say nothing about any particular person having done it—
unless you wish to employ a private detective. Just collect
your insurance, and let that company do the worrying."

Marriott groaned. He opened his mouth and panted like
a dog on a hot day. Dr. Andrews, who still was in atten-
dance, frowned at Connor, evidently wishing the police
would leave.

"It's going to be—hard to believe—especially to the
insurance company," said Marriott between gasps for air,
"But the money—means next to nothing. Those Ming
urns, not to mention—smaller pieces—were the largest
and finest in the world. They are irreplaceable. Money isn't."

"Not for some people, maybe," admitted Connor with
a shrug.

Impressed by the size of the collector's loss, Connor got
in touch with the station, asking whether any word had
come from the radio patrol cars or the State troopers, who
had been rushed to the roadways of Nassau County to
intercept suspicious-seeming strangers.

The result was as vacant as a yawn. Nothing had been heard.

By daylight then, Connor and all his men went over the grounds and then the moderate-sized but beautiful house a second time.

"I'm sorry, Mr. Marriott," he said regretfully, when all he could think of to do had been done. The old collector was in pyjamas and lounging robe now, lying down. He had recovered from his threatened attack, but had been advised to avoid all stress for several days. The advice was impossible for a man like Ralph Marriott to obey.

"I tell you, it's the work of that scoundrel Tomeroy!" snarled Marriott, chewing his lower lip. "He bid me up to the blue sky, before he'd give up those Mings. D'you mean to say it isn't plain to you?"

"I'm afraid not, Mr. Marriott," admitted Connor wearily. "You said a while back that this man, Josiah Tomeroy, was a rival collector you beat out for some choice pieces—"

"Yeh!" snapped Marriott, a momentary rasping chuckle of remembered triumph coming before he frowned again. "Damned old fool. Lives in Scarsdale. He was so mad he threw a catalogue at me—right down in the Yancey Galleries! So of course this is his sneaking idea of getting even. Nobody else in the world would have any motive for destroying antique porcelains, just because I had them. Oh, hell, it was Tomeroy."

"Unless you get some kind of evidence, you'd better keep still about Tomeroy," Connor said bluntly. "There are libel laws, you know. Until we know a lot more, the police can do nothing. And you'd better not try!"

"Why you—you *cop!*"

Rage and stinging contempt flared up, as Marriott bounced out of bed, disregarding his doctor's instructions. "Come here, fall down on your two-for-a-nickel job, and then try to tell me what to do?

"Why, dammit, I'll show you up, Connor!" he snarled, banging a clenched fist into the palm of his left hand. "I'll hire a private dick. This man Jigger Masters. He showed you up once, and I'll have him do it again."

"Oh, no! You wouldn't go and do that," protested Connor, with admirably simulated shock.

Ralph Marriott was thumbing rapidly through the Long Island phone directory.

Lieutenant Selwyn Connor preserved his facial expression of shock and humiliation, until he had the door closed behind him. Then he chuckled, and his stooped figure straightened.

"Maybe we'll have some fun here after all," he grinned at Detective Sergeant Emerson, who was standing disconsolately at the front door. "The old man's calling in Jigger Masters. I was just about to suggest that, when he thought of it his own self."

2

SHROUD OF COMEDY

J.C.K. MASTERS WAS in a shower when Mitsui, his Jap servant, answered the phone. There had been two fast sets of pre-breakfast tennis with Marshall Vandervoort.

The good-natured youth was taking his defeat philosophically. He lazied in a lukewarm tub. After which he would eat some of Mitsui's fluffy scrambled eggs and crisp bacon, before driving home. There his extremely personable young bride would be awaiting him. But for the objections of this same bride to becoming a widow, Marsh Vandervoort would have been an active assistant to Jigger Masters.

"Man on phone," squealed Mitsui, to make himself heard above the rush of the needle shower. "He snap, chew his mustache, mebbe bite me if can. Says name allasame Ma'yot. Mebbe new client, I dunno."

"Malliot?" guessed Jigger, turning off the water and reaching for a big towel. "Don't know him. If he's a client though, he's King of the Cannibal Isles, with me. Just two shakes of a dead lamb's tail—"

As he was speaking, he used the Turkish towel. Then binding it about his lean waist, he strode into the bedroom, and through this to the desk phone in the living room he used as an office.

"Masters talking," he announced with pleasant expectancy.

He sat down in the desk swivel chair, and reached one-handedly for a paper packet of cigarettes and a box of matches.

"Why, sure, Mr. Marriott, that's my business," he said after a moment. "It sounds like a hunt in Scarsdale—after I've had a look-see at your home. Hard to tell, from the bare facts you give... Oh-h... let's say five hundred dollars retainer. The fee, naturally is proportional to the work involved. Never excessive, though. Yes. All right. I'll be over in about one hour."

He replaced the receiver, arose, and went into the next room for clean linen. Marsh Vandervoort, his tanned visage expressing languid curiosity, came in, toweling his spine.

"Want to spend an hour at the Metropolitan Museum of Art—and then an afternoon at the Public Library?" asked Masters, his hazel eyes alight with anticipation.

Vandervoort shrugged. "What's wrong, a new murder in Gomorrah?"

"No, not murder. Only a sort of comedy—thus far, anyhow."

In a few words the detective told him of the vandalism at Marriott's. Then:

"Of course I know a little about ceramics in a general way. What I'd like to have you do, Marsh, is learn all there is to know about Ming porcelains. All the superficial stuff, anyhow. Latest news, theories, and such. I believe there's some kind of secret connected with the glaze on that particular pottery."

"That's right," confirmed Vandervoort cheerfully.

"Dot—my wife—has a little Ming vase. It's about three inches tall, and it's insured for $750! It's nearly all in the crack glaze, she tells me. No one in the whole world, not even the Chinkies themselves, can make that sort of thing now. Lost art." He grinned, and pulled clean clothes out of a suitcase. "Do we eat now?" he asked. "Dot will be stirring pretty soon now, and finding nothing but a dented pillow next to her...."

Dressing rapidly, they ate with excellent appetite the breakfast Mitsui offered.

Masters phoned Tom Gildersleeve, his chunky, red-faced assistant, who had rooms in a private home in Mineola.

"What I want you to do right away, Tom," said Masters, after he had repeated tersely the facts told by Marriott—and the accusation against the rival collector, Josiah Tomeroy, "is get up to Scarsdale as quickly as you can. Check on Tomeroy for last night and this morning."

PRYDE ESTATES, IN which Marriott's home and landscaped halfacre were situated, was a hilly and wooded tract just westward of the south end of Biskra Bay, Marriott's family consisted of himself, his young-appearing fifty-year-old wife, and a semi-invalid sister three years older than himself. Except for world travel, and the ex-steelman's prized collections, the three lived quietly enough, showing few signs to casual acquaintances of Marriott's substantial wealth.

Sergeant Emerson evidently was on the lookout for Masters, for as Mitsui drove the detective's car up the winding bluestone drive, he came out and waved, then immediately disappeared inside the house. Lieutenant

Connor came out then, with the amiable little sergeant following.

Connor's face was grave, but he winked portentously as he came down to the car.

"I'm judged and found wanting, Jigger," he sighed. "Old Marriott insisted on calling you. Officially, you understand, I'm sore as hell. Privately—well, put 'er there." He extended his hand for a brisk, cordial shake.

"I suppose this is really what Marriott thinks—a private war between collectors?" asked Masters, as they walked quickly up to the house. "No signs of theft, he said."

"Scarcely any time, except maybe to snatch one or two pieces and run," agreed Connor, frowning. "I dunno. You'll maybe find a whole lot of clues; but to me it's just as hard to read as—as hog-Latin. Dynamiting what they couldn't grab wasn't a usual stunt of thieves in my day, though. I s'pose maybe Marriott's right about it being Tomeroy. Some of these rich old cranks are peevish as all hell, when you dance up and down on their pet bunions. Marriott himself might have thought up a stunt like this, I should say, if it'd been Tomeroy who got the bric-à-brac...."

The last words died out in a mutter, as they entered the cheerful, somewhat ornately furnished downstairs hall.

"Come right in this way," bade a croaking bass voice. Marriott had dispensed with servants while the police were running in and out. He was in the first room at the left, a living room and library, beyond which French doors gave upon a glassed sun porch.

Marriott, his pudgy figure wrapped in a lounging robe of undyed pongee, half-inclined in a chaise-longue obviously brought in from the porch. Its gay crimson and yellow clashed with the more somber, rich furnishings of the room.

Masters stepped in, and shook hands, holding the clasp for a few seconds while he sought a complete impression of his new employer.

Here was a fighter, he decided. Ralph Marriott was sturdily built. In his youth and young manhood he had been a smiling, bulldog-jawed throw-back in a family of aristocrats. He had liked to box. He had liked the bustle and fierce strife of moneymaking. And none of these had done him any harm.

Even now he still played a sharp game of handball. And in spite of transferring his interests from steel mergers to travel and the collection of art objects, he was able and two-fisted. That was what made his present disability annoy him so much.

"I don't know for the life of me what those thugs did," he growled, as Masters put him back on the chaise-longue, gazing sharply at a suggestion of bluish tint that showed in the firm lips.

"Ever since they put that smothering bag over my head, I've been unable to breathe right! Feel like I was choking—down here." And he pounded one fist on his broad chest.

"Hm," said Masters. "Ever have any heart trouble? Any vertigo or faintness?"

"Never," said Marriott. "Oh, don't bother about me. I had a thorough going-over less than a month ago, just to be on the safe side. Dr. Strake"—he named one of the most famous diagnosticians in New York City—"told me I was sound in wind and limb, that my heart was as good as it ever had been.

"Dr. Andrews, my wife's physician, just went over the machinery again today. He seemed worried until he made his examination. Then he said I ought to live to be a hundred."

Masters nodded. There was something that did not look exactly right, in Marriott's color. Still, these two were good doctors. Doubtless Marriott was sound enough.

"Just take it easy, then, Mr. Marriott," said Masters quietly. "You gave me an admirable summary of events over the phone. Now I'm going to look for myself. Afterward I'll have a few questions to ask."

"Ask 'em now," barked Marriott, glaring disagreeably at Connor, who kept his glance averted. "These damn flatfeet will have spoiled anything like a clue, even supposing there was one. What do you want to know?"

"Well—" The detective hesitated, about to follow Connor toward the galleries. "Did you smell anything peculiar? Were these men ordinary roughnecks, or—"

"Smell!" snorted Marriott. "My Lord in Heaven! With that bag over my head? It must have been used to carry very ripe limburger, or dead cats, or something like that. I had Lane—the butler, that is—take it out and burn it. No, I couldn't smell anything else—"

"You *burned* that bag?" Masters straightened, frowning. "For goodness sake, Connor, get after it. If any part of it is left, bring it to me. Why—well, look, anyhow. See the butler immediately."

"Now what?" growled Marriott. "It was just a dirty cloth bag. The sort an old-fashioned rag-picker carried. Why, what's wrong with burning it? I felt as though the filth of it had got all the way down into my lungs."

Masters shook his head grimly. No use to cry over spilt milk. He went out.

HE BEGAN A swift, thorough examination of the scene of the attack and dynamiting.

Beginning with the jimmied window through which the intruders had entered, the detective painstakingly went over the course of the scorch left by the burned fuse. While he was still at the window, Connor returned.

"Not a damn scrap, Jigger!" he said disgustedly. "They've got a big incinerator in the basement, and it's still warm. I've taken out all the ashes, and there isn't a piece of anything as big as your toenail, unburned. I've saved the ashes, if you want to look at them."

"I will, later," frowned Masters. "Look at the latch of this window. An easy job—if you have that particular tool."

He pointed out that the only indication of forcing came at the upper sash. The window was not tight. A space of perhaps one-sixty-fourth of an inch lay between the two cross-sashes. The stock latch was located on the inner sash, a slanting flange being moved into a slot on the outer sash by a thumb lever.

"Simply pushed the blade of a thin, strong knife up here, between the two. Then one sharp blow drove the knife against the flange—and presto! The rest was easy."

"Trusting souls, these millionaires," said Connor. "Why, dammit, any garage mechanic with maybe twenty bucks' worth of plated silver in the dining room'd lock up better'n that!"

On the ground outside the grass had been trampled; but there were no distinct footprints. And though Masters went over every inch of floor surface where the intruders might have trod, he found nothing.

"Workmanlike job in the modern manner. Nothing for us, except the fact that they used dynamite, and a rather special sort of fast fuse. Call New York City, Connor, and ask headquarters to make queries," concluded Masters, when they were in the ruined gallery. "They'll be in touch with all the blasting supply houses in this area. There's no hope of tracing mere dynamite, since many a farm in Connecticut uses it constantly. But fast fuse—the kind called 'instantaneous,' is rare. I'd like to know where anybody could buy it."

Save for rescuing a few pieces found intact in the debris, nothing had been done to clean up the mess in the ceramics gallery. Jigger Masters measured the broken wall, to get a clear idea of the explosion. Patently the destruction had been caused by a small charge, probably no more than a single stick, equipped with detonator and fuse.

There was a wheezing sound behind him. He straightened, and saw the owner, Marriott in the doorway. The man was in a queer, arresting attitude. One hand reached above his head, to grasp the cross-wise lintel, while the other hand was pressed to the left side of his chest.

He croaked, trying to talk, but his gasps for air interrupted.

"Here!" said Masters in a startled voice. "You must lie down, Mr. Marriott. Heavens, you look as if—"

He broke off short and sprang to catch the millionaire. Marriott let go his hold on the lintel, his fingernails scratching audibly like a cat's claws. He slumped, knees bending forward. Off balance himself, all the detective could do was to ease the fall to the floor, and then prop up the man's head.

A strangled, awful sound escaped Marriott. One good look at the man's congested face, and the detective yelled for assistance. Down the stairs pattered two elderly women, followed by three servants from the floor above.

"Bring me some brandy! And call your doctor back immediately! Brandy first."

But Ralph Marriott passed beyond human aid in the next half minute. Despite the almost frantic ministrations of Masters, the two women, and the aid of the servants, a series of gasping convulsions seized the collector.

Then, with Masters lifting his straining chest up from the floor in a vain effort of easing that awesome struggle for air, the end came. Marriott slumped. After two quick tests, lifting the eyelid, and then holding his watch crystal to the blue lips, Masters slowly rose to his feet.

"It's no use, Mrs. Marriott," he said sadly to the weeping woman. "Your husband is dead!"

3

THE SAFFRON HORROR

DR. ANDREWS RETURNED hurriedly. He turned pale, and was manifestly astounded when he made certain Marriott was dead.

"Why, I—I don't see how on earth such a thing could have happened," he almost whispered. "Marriott was in the best of health. This shock ought not to have bothered him one bit. I just can't believe it!"

"Well, stay here," said Masters soberly. "See to the women, and try to convince them that an autopsy is necessary. They will hate it, of course, but I am depending on you, doctor. Right now I'm going over to the district attorney and get an order. This looks as bad to me as it does to you."

Masters rode with Mitsui directly to Mineola. There he found that Casimir Sterling was away, but was expected back in an hour. Dr. Cortelyou, Medical Examiner for Nassau County, was there, however.

Masters sent him on ahead, stating that he would bring the autopsy order a little later.

"Food is indicated," Masters told his chauffeur-factotum, Mitsui. "Drive back to our place, and see what you can hustle together that's edible. It may be a long time before another meal."

Ten minutes later they were in the Biskra Harbor house.
There Mitsui swiftly and efficiently sliced cold roast beef
and Liederkranz cheese, and set out a cold bottle of Pilsner.
Mitsui was just pouring a cup of black coffee when the
phone rang.

It was Marshall Vandervoort on the wire.

"Just picked up a bit of gossip at the Metropolitan,
Chief," he drawled. "Thought you might be interested to
know. There was a Japanese, name of Ichiara Kagodi, fell
out of a plane, last night, some time. Or early this morning. Accident happened up somewhere near Worcester,
Massachusetts. Itchy was on his way to Boston.

"The reason why you might want to know more was just
this. Itchy was well known to people who handle pottery
of the expensive sort. Kind of a middleman or broker, I
reckon. It was he, for instance, who sold the Ming porcelains to the Yancey Galleries—the Ming urns and vases
which Marriott bought, you understand. And now he's
dead, Suicide they say, though accident was within the
realm of possibility."

"How did you happen to hear?" Masters' question was
sharp.

"Eh? Oh, I've been chatting here. Dot and I are
acquainted with the Curator. This Jap, Itchy, has turned
up a number of antique porcelains which the Metropolitan experts didn't even know or believe existed. So they
kept an eye on him."

"They *were* genuine antiques—the ones he brought to
light?"

"Oh, heck, yes. The Museum people examined them.
Then, of course, they began to hope that the Yancey Galler-

ies would sell the lot to somebody who'd donate them to the Met. But not Ralph Marriott. I just wondered if there was something spooky about those Ming antiques."

Masters made a noncommittal sound. "Thus far the only crime we know about is the destruction of some valuable, insured property," he reminded the young man. "It probably could be argued that the attack on Marriott caused his death; but that would be a point for lawyers and medical experts. Always providing, of course, that the post mortem reveals nothing beyond a bad heart, or something of the kind.

"But that was good scouting, Marsh. I wish you'd find out whatever you can from New York, about Ichiara's trip to Boston. Where the body has been taken, and so forth, There may be some connection between that happening and the raid on Marriott's place. We may want to follow up in a hurry, just a little bit later."

The detective finished up his coffee then, and returned thoughtfully to his car. He was wishing, on the drive back to Mineola and Sterling's office, that Tom Gildersleeve, sent out to check on the movements of Josiah Tomeroy at Scarsdale, would phone or bring in a report soon, If that rival collector actually had been the criminal, much elaborate investigation which right now seemed on the cards, would be futile.

"But I'll be darned if it looks to me like a spite case. The feel of it is too serious," reflected Masters.

Casimir Sterling was in. The district attorney bore no love whatever for Jigger Masters. The detective had made Sterling look a trifle foolish on one previous occasion, and the district attorney was not a big enough man to shrug and forget it.

But by that very same token, Casimir Sterling was willing—nay, eager—to let Masters go ahead now and put his foot in it. He concealed a gleam of the eyes when Masters bluntly put forward his suspicions of murder, and immediately signed an autopsy order.

"You understand," said Sterling, "that this is entirely on your own responsibility. If it proves a mare's nest—"

Masters hastened to his car, and ordered Mitsui to return as speedily as possible to Pryde Estates, where Cortelyou probably had completed his preliminary examination.

THE TRUTH WAS that Dr. Richard Cortelyou was just having the creepiest experience of his entire medical career.

He talked to Dr. Andrews, who had stayed at Marriott's, and then mounted the stairs to the chamber where the body had been placed: A lighted cigar was between his teeth. At this moment, in spite of Andrews' evident perturbation, the medical examiner supposed this would be just a routine job. Masters had not waited to explain much.

There was only the dead man and his sister, the dried-up Esther Marriott in the room, yellow-skinned; stiffly upright in a straight chair, she sat, regarding the sheet-covered corpse. She turned a stony glare upon the intruding medical examiner.

"Should think you might let a body rest in peace!" she snapped.

Cortelyou did not answer at once. He extinguished his cigar, and sighed. Then gently he persuaded the woman to leave the room. All alike, these relatives. What difference did it make to any dead man, whether or not an autopsy was performed upon his inert clay?

He drew away the sheet, and looked down upon all that was left of Ralph Marriott. Cortelyou began to frown slightly. Not much shrinkage or collapse visible, he thought to himself. Kind of odd color in the face, too. Masters had said it was blue—cyanosed. Now it didn't look that way. Rather it was waxy, yellow! Cortelyou looked closely at that. He had never seen exactly this hue in the skin of a dead man. *Bright* yellow, you might say!

He reached over intending to remove the rest of the clothing. He took hold of Marriott's right arm, intending to flex it out of the way....

Instantly a smothered oath burst from his lips, and he leaped back a pace. Then for a space of ten seconds he stood, staring down, and rubbing his own hands on his waistcoat as if to rid them of some contamination.

Shrinkage? Collapse? There was none at all.

And it felt to Dr. Cortelyou as though the skin of the dead man somehow had distended! The arm was straight, and already gripped by the strangest phenomenon Cortelyou had ever seen.

"A sort of *springy* rigor!" he breathed. "Now, what in the blue blazes could cause a thing like that?"

He bent down suddenly to a more thorough examination. And as he worked the look of horror grew deeper in his eyes!

There came a thumping on the door. Miss Esther Marriott was demanding in her shrill, quavering treble that the medical examiner go away, and take the police with him.

The medical examiner, however, was telephoning, talking to Lieutenant Conner.

"I tell you, *there's something ghastly happening right now to the corpse!*" whispered Cortelyou in conclusion, and hung up the house phone. He wiped beads of perspiration from his forehead, then rapidly pulled back the sheet so it covered the remains.

When Masters knocked, and was recognized, Cortelyou rather breathlessly opened the door, grasped the detective by the wrist, and drew him in, closing and locking the door again.

"Thank the Lord you're here! Did you get it?" almost whispered the physician. "You had an idea, all right, Jigger! But what do you *know?* What *is* this damned thing that got Marriott?"

Masters answered the flood of questions by simply stating that the police ambulance was downstairs, waiting outside. If the body was ready they would call stretcher men and take it.

"What's got under your skin, Doctor?" he asked. "You seem to have developed a few suspicions yourself!"

"Suspicions!" The word was shakily scornful. "You—you pull back the sheet! I'll snap the electric light on for just a half minute!"

A tumult of questioning and weird supposition swept through the detective's mind. After one quizzical glance at the disturbed medico, he stepped across the soft rug to the four-poster bed where Marriott lay.

Was it sheer imagination, yet did it seem, even before he pulled down the white covering, that the form beneath the linen somehow had *bulged,* grown puffy and monstrous?

Masters felt his own scalp bristle, and tingly chills race down to the tips of his fingers. With a quick motion he threw back the sheet. Then he started, and gasped involuntarily.

"Oh—great God!"

This was awe and horror, with no thought of blasphemy. As quickly as he had pulled away the sheet, Masters threw it back into place. He stepped away, face pale, and beads of cold perspiration sprang instantly to his forehead.

"This is hellish!" he said. "Go see if Andrews has left. I think I glimpsed him downstairs, with Mrs. Marriott. We're not going to take this body over to Mineola, after all. If I were in your shoes, I'd put up a quarantine notice immediately. Leave it there until we're sure this thing isn't—catching!"

As the medical examiner went out of the room, Jigger went to a window and threw it open, breathing in great gusts of cool air. The horrible job of autopsy would have to be conducted in this very room, lest some unknown, fearful plague be loosed upon Long Island!

A DELAY ENSUED, before Cortelyou was ready to start. But when he returned with his instruments the ambulance men had made ready the body. The medical examiner was calm and collected now. This might prove to be some new and frightful malady; but if so it was his business to find out the fact, so others might be protected. He went to work with the same cool precision he would have exercised had he been probing for a bullet.

Jigger Masters and Andrews stayed apart until all was ready. Then they drew near, with difficulty repressing gasps as they saw the body again. Andrews caught nervously at Jigger's arm.

The corpse had changed greatly for the worse. The skin of Marriott's entire body now was definitely yellow!

And that was not the worst of it. Just as if liquid under high pressure had been forced into the veins of the dead man the corpse had bulged! His eyes had popped open!

The thorough job took a full hour. There was not a scratch or cut of any description—not even a perceptible pin-prick—on any part of Ralph Marriott. This fact made Masters himself pace the floor, scowling. It seemed to upset his first tentative theory, that the man had been poisoned without knowing it.

At the first incision of the scalpel, a cry of disbelief and horror came even from the medical examiner.

All through the tissues laid open, growing in every vein and artery was a saffron tangle which looked like yellow seaweed or fungus!

Jigger Masters was pale, but grimly self-contained. "That's no natural malady, is it, gentlemen?" he asked.

"Never heard of such a thing!" said Cortelyou decidedly. "Did you, Andrews?"

"Hm," considered the little man. "I'd have to have notice of that question. Seems to me I did… long ago… an Oriental ailment. It's embolism of a kind, isn't it? The heart valve is choked up like a sink-trap full of wool wire! And the brain…! I suppose, though, that growth in the finer blood vessels did not come until well after death."

Masters was inwardly excited, but seemed collected. "You'll have to make allowances for a layman, gentlemen," he said. "To my naked eye this stuff that has grown all through the blood vessels looks like some fine-stranded seaweed."

"Section slides under the mike will tell us, I think," Cortelyou said, "I never saw anything in the nature of this precise virulent yellow. At a guess I'd say the stuff was either a rare form of alga—that's pond scum, not to put too fine a degree of definition on it—or else some saprophytic growth like the familiar antler-fungus. They are not vastly different. Both grow with such terrific speed that the growth can be watched with no more magnification than a mere hand lens."

"But both of those depend on decaying matter for their food," objected Andrews tartly. "They wouldn't grow inside a living man."

"Umm." Cortelyou was silent, frowning. "There's plenty broken-down animal and vegetable matter carried in the blood stream," he said. "Only...."

"I think the stuff is growing faster and faster right now!" said Masters softly but with tense emphasis. "I want you to make slides of it, Cortelyou, and find out its nature without delay. Somehow it got inside Ralph Marriott, started to grow with hideous swiftness, killed him, and then kept on growing until he was actually *stuffed!* Ralph Marriott was my client. I feel now in honor bound to discover who murdered him, and how. Perhaps we know the reason why—and again perhaps not.

"If you'll excuse me, gentlemen, I'm going to make a flying trip to Scarsdale. One of my assistants is up there; but this development makes speed necessary. I am going to tackle a man who just possibly may have hated Ralph Marriott enough to kill him in this subtle fashion."

"I'll carry on, Jigger. Let me know as soon as possible," nodded Lieutenant Connor gravely. He walked close to Masters and spoke in a subdued voice—"you'd better hurry if you want to do anything your own self. You and I—well, *we've been exposed!*"

4

THE RIVAL COLLECTOR

PARKING HIS FLIVVER at the Scarsdale station Tom Gildersleeve made inquiries. He found out that Josiah Tomeroy, the man whom Marriott had accused, was well if not favorably known. His home was atop the cliff which, just south of the railway station, overhung the automobile road known as the Bronx Parkway. Up there, as Gildersleeve immediately discovered, was a small but excellently built brick-and-stucco cottage, set in the heavily wooded park through which the residence streets wound.

Smoking his chocolate-colored meerschaum, Gildersleeve went up to the grounds to reconnoiter. And he chanced to overhear an altercation which his shrewdness helped him to use.

Near the back door a fat woman, probably part Negress, was arguing sulkily with a thinnish, irascible old man in a lounging robe. The woman had a market basket on her arm, but she seemed reluctant to leave.

"Ah tell yo', I cain't do ev'ything!" was her final word. Then she turned, muttering to herself, and started downhill toward the small business section of Scarsdale.

Gildersleeve joined the woman a moment later.

"Works you pretty hard, doesn't he?" he asked sympathetically.

For a moment the woman, whose name a little later was divulged as Pearl White, seemed about to explode in wrath. But Tom chuckled disarmingly. "An old devil, isn't he?" he asked.

Pearl was willing enough to talk to someone. She came mornings to do just the cleaning, usually. Josiah Tomeroy kept a Chinese servant, Li Gow. But last night Li Gow had vanished, supposedly to White Plains, where he had a brother. Tomeroy insisted on Pearl staying and doing the marketing and cooking also, until the Oriental returned.

Her complaint, though it mattered little, was the fact that she had drawn an advance on her wages. And now Tomeroy refused her any further advance unless she stayed and helped him out in emergency.

"Him an' all his fancy plates an' vases!" she complained. "Ah'll get me anothah job."

Gildersleeve kept right with her until she entered a meat market. Then he returned to the house on the cliff.

"Pretty tough customer at that!" he reflected. "But there isn't any way Pearl could tell whether or not he'd been out on Long Island last night. Mebbe I'd better brace him."

He decided to wait around until the cleaning woman returned, at any rate. It was simple to hide in the shrubbery, keeping an eye on the house. He hoped for another glimpse of Tomeroy, but in this he was disappointed.

A few minutes later Pearl returned with her purchases, and went inside. Then, just as Gildersleeve knocked out his pipe, intending to go to the front door, a brougham came to a stop in the street opposite Tomeroy's. Gildersleeve watched interestedly, for at first glance he had seen that the occupants of the car were Chinese.

Could they be bringing back the missing Li Gow?

Three Chinese got out, and walked briskly to the front door. They were dressed somewhat alike, in blue serge suits, black-and-white oxfords, and straw hats with fancy bands. Whether or not one was the missing servant, Tom could not guess. Possibly they were relatives. Something like an accident might have happened to the missing Chink....

Tom Gildersleeve settled down on a bench, and relighted his pipe. The Chinese interested him, but he could see no probable connection with his own investigation. Soon as the visitors left he would have it out with Tomeroy himself.

That moment Gil came up with a start. A familiar figure had come past on foot, looking up at the house. Jigger Masters!

"Hey, chief, I'm here," called Gildersleeve. Masters stopped, then nodded. He came to the assistant's place of concealment.

"Hell's broken loose," Masters said briefly. "Did you get a chance to find out anything about Tomeroy? Marriott's dead, and it looks as though murder was certain. I—"

He got no further. An upstairs window slammed open, and from it projected the head and waving bare arms of a swarthy fat Negress. Her crinkly hair was bound in a white cloth.

"Halp! Halp!" she yelled lustily, bawling the words with her mouth opened to its widest extent. "Halp! Po-leece!" As if that effort exhausted her strength, she vanished. Masters had caught sight of her just in time to see her go.

"She fainted, I think," he snapped.

At a run he started for the front door, but he was not

fated to reach it just then. Out of it burst three men in a hurry, and Gildersleeve shouted. These were the Chinese.

Masters brought up short. He saw the narrowed, glittering black eyes of the trio turned squarely upon him.

But both Gildersleeve and he were caught off guard. The three Chinamen brought hands from the side pockets of their jackets. Stubby automatic pistols, levelled at Masters and Gildersleeve.

"Go back, you," squealed the foremost Oriental, gesturing toward the shrubbery of the garden. "Quick—or you die!"

There could be no argument, though Gildersleeve growled and seemed to bristle. One of the Chinese got into the car, starting the motor, the other two kept weapons levelled, and both detectives were forced to walk backwards slowly. Then at a sharp command the Chinese turned, leaped into the brougham. The car started with a lurch, quickly accelerated, and vanished down the winding road through the woods. Masters scribbled down the number, though he doubted it would be of any use.

He did not wait for explanations, but dashed for the front door which was standing open.

"Call the police first, Gil," he commanded. "Then see to the woman upstairs."

For himself he kept to the matter of the collector, Josiah Tomeroy. A shivery hunch had come to him.

One look into the richly furnished living room brought grim confirmation. A cry burst from Masters' lips, and he darted forward to kneel on the rug.

Here, sprawled limply across a low ottoman, face downward, was a thin-framed old man in a dressing gown, unconscious from a swelling bruise on the back of his head.

5

SIX HOURS TO LIVE

IT WAS JOSIAH Tomeroy, of course. The terrified Negress, Pearl White, assured them of that as soon as she could be coaxed downstairs.

Then turmoil ensued. The Scarsdale police came, extremely suspicious at first of Masters and Gildersleeve. It was not until Sergeant Brett of Scarsdale heard Masters' hurried recital of the events in Marriott's home on Long Island, and put in a call to Mineola for verification, that the two detectives were accepted.

A physician revived Tomeroy without difficulty. He complained of a headache, but that was all for the time being. Masters decided to give him a few more minutes to recover before demanding the story of the three Chinese.

From the rug Jigger Masters had picked up a printed card. It read as follows:

SOCIETY OF FICTILE ARTISANS

Peiping, China

American representatives:

Messrs. Chan, Soy & Ling

726 Hudson Street

New York, N.Y.

"The track's getting hot, Gil," said Masters grimly. "I wonder if Tomeroy had anything destroyed by those Chinese? They just *might* have been the very ones who did for Marriott!"

"Wouldn't wonder at all, chief," said Gildersleeve. "There's been somep'n smashed all to powder out here." He jerked a thumb toward an adjoining room. "Pearl White heard it goin' on, an' come down. They grabbed at her, but she got away an' run upstairs. That was when we heard her yell. They were poundin' on her door, tryin' to shut her up. She keeled over."

Masters nodded, and went back to where Sergeant Brett, a police detective, and a doctor were grouped around Josiah Tomeroy. He was snarling with rage. Now he leaped up, throwing aside the doctor's restraining arm, and dashed to the next room, a sort of library in which were set cases containing antique pottery.

His shrill scream of poignant loss told the story. His one greatest possession, a gigantic Ming urn for which he had paid $50,000 only three days earlier, had been smashed to shards—and many of these fragments pounded to powder!

Masters paled. This so far was a repetition of what had happened at Marriott's. The detective wasted no time. He seized the doctor by the arm and drew him aside, telling in swift, brutal sentences what he feared might happen to Josiah Tomeroy if the parallel continued good.

"I don't know what it means, Doctor, but watch Tomeroy closely! It would horrify but not surprise me if right now he had some of that awful fungus in his veins!"

"Oh, but I don't see any signs of anything like that," protested the medico. "And even if I did—" He shrugged.

"Perhaps no one could stop it!" agreed Masters. "No one alive. But watch! If the same thing happens here, Tomeroy will die approximately six hours after he was assaulted! One of those hours has passed. Go now and stay with him. If he starts to breathe asthmatically—"

With a smothered exclamation the doctor turned away again to the patient. Masters got hold of Gildersleeve. He tendered the business card of the "Society of Fictile Artisans."

"This gives us a hint," said Masters savagely. "It means pottery, porcelains, things like that. Take this card. Look up the New York phone or street directory. If there's a phone there, find out what you can. If there really are Chinese in business there, call Centre Street and ask McDonald to send a squad car. Have him hold every yellow man he finds there!"

"All right, Chief. I sent that number of the brougham. The radio patrol cars are looking for it now. They say the plates weren't issued for that make, though. One of them foreign cars—a Minerva—"

"O Lord, Gil, this has got me nervous as a cat. We can't know until it's too late, but we'll just have to work as well as we can by telephone until we know about Tomeroy."

"You mean—him too?" almost whispered Gildersleeve, his ruddy color fading.

"Yes! Of course it may not be so. But I swear I imagine I can hear him breathing hard, right now. You go do what I said. Then when that's done, call Mineola and Connor at Pryde Estates. See if anything has happened. Tell Connor about this."

WAITING PROVED A ghastly nightmare. Masters heard

Tomeroy's simple enough story, as soon as the man calmed down. Except in one crucial point, it added nothing to their knowledge.

He admitted the quarrel with Marriott, but shrugged contemptuously at the suggestion that he might have had anything to do with the vandalism and death.

"I won't even try to answer that," he snorted. "Here is the same thing, over again—as far as the smashing of a valuable Ming vase is concerned. An urn, I should say. To think of what I paid for it. And how I had to positively chase that Jap, in order to get it!"

"Jap?" asked Masters. Here was a new facet, though it linked up rapidly with something he had heard from Marshall Vandervoort.

"Yes, that damned little bloodsucker, Ichiara Kagodi," answered Tomeroy, gritting his teeth. "He sold the original collection of Mings—the ones on which Marriott outbid me—to the Yancey Galleries.

"When I was stung by Marriott I went after Kagodi myself. And he *did* have one more big urn! Intended to keep it for himself. I had to pay $50,000 to get it! And now—oh Lord!"

Masters stared at him fascinated, a chill of horror creeping up and down the detective's spine. Was Tomeroy wheezing asthmatically, or was it sheer imagination? Masters glanced at the doctor, and saw him looking intently, frowning a little.

The detective turned away. There was nothing to do but wait, though waiting was increasingly awful. Masters bit his lip. Kagodi! That was the name of the man Marshall Vandervoort had told him had fallen from a plane, up somewhere near Worcester, Massachusetts. Could there be any connection?

Gildersleeve came to the door of the room and beckoned. Masters was glad to join him.

"The old run-around, chief," said Gil briefly. "A brick apartment house at 726 Hudson. No Chinks there. Never have been. Guess they were all fixed up—fake address, stolen plates—"

"Of course. Still, three Chinese in a car," frowned Masters. "Seems like one of those radio patrols ought to pick 'em up. Good Lord, I wish we could get back to Mineola. This case may be similar, but I'm retained by Marriott—"

"Oh, say, chief," broke in Gildersleeve. "I got Mineola. There wasn't anything new with Connor. But Marsh Vandervoort has been trying to get you. He's down at the Metropolitan. You can get him at the Curator's private number. Here it is." He held out a penciled slip which Masters took.

"Marsh is all hot and buttered up like a piece of toast," said Gil with a final grin.

Masters did not answer. He went directly to the phone in the hall and got the connection. And in a short time he learned that his young assistant had cause for excitement indeed. Marsh had stumbled upon something which bore only too grimly on this very puzzle of Marriott—and possibly Tomeroy!

"There's something horrible about this, Jigger!" he almost shouted on the phone. " 'Member I told you about that Jap, Ichiara Kagodi? The fella who sold those Mings, and then who fell out of a plane up near Worcester?"

"Yes, take it easy," cautioned Masters. "What happened?" But before the other spoke, Masters was certain that he knew.

"That Jap, Itchy, was fleeing for his life! He'd got into some kind of a jam in New York, so the pilot understood, and grabbed a taxi. He got out to Roosevelt Field, hired a plane for the night flight to Boston, and fairly jumped and wheezed around while they were warming up a bus. He—"

"*Wheezed*, you say?" broke in Masters, with a peculiar inflection of voice.

"Asthma, probably. Anyhow, Lee Wilson—that's the pilot—said he was so done up he c'd hardly get his breath. But he was all wild to get off the ground, and away. Pulled out a big roll of bills, and paid in advance.

"But he didn't seem to be able to sit still, even when they got up in the air. He was squirming around in the cockpit, pulling at his collar. He'd unsnapped the safety belt, it seems. All of a sudden he leaped up, right while Wilson was banking the monoplane to the east. Itchy went right over, kicking and seeming to grab at his own throat—"

"Acted like he was smothering?" asked Masters sharply.

"Something like that. Wilson, of course, was thunderstruck. He couldn't land very near, because the Jap's body had fallen in an apple orchard. But he got down somehow on the fairway of a golf course about a mile away, and ran back as fast as he could. Itchy was dead, of course. Pretty badly smashed.

"But the latest news from the morgue at Westboro is what I wanted to tell you. They think now that Itchy didn't die from the airplane fall. His body is all bloated up. It looks like poison."

FOR A SPACE of three seconds Masters was silent. "I see," he said slowly. "All right, Marsh, that's excellent work, and you're on the right track, without a doubt. Marriott's body showed the same symptoms."

"What?" shouted Vandervoort.

"I can't talk now over the phone," said the detective. "I wish you and your nice wife would take a short airplane hop, though. You *might* save somebody's life. Listen carefully now, Marsh. We don't know yet what this devilish stuff is; but it is almost sure to be some kind of a murder instrument.

"Fly to Westboro, tell the coroner up there to look for something like yellow seaweed grown all through the veins and arteries. Then have him get in touch with me or Dr. Cortelyou, through the Mineola police station.

"And ask him to keep the story out of the papers for a day or two, if he can. It might cause a plague-panic—though I doubt very much that it is an illness at all, in the ordinary sense of the word."

"You mean a—a—"

"I'd only be guessing," cut in Masters. "But what I want you to tell that coroner is that until the nature of this is determined finally, he and his assistants had better use rubber gloves in handling the body of that Jap. And you—well, you'd better call me long distance, or leave word at Mineola for me, if anything new cracks up there."

"I'll do it, chief," said Marsh. "We'll be leaving Newark in an hour or less. Bye!"

Masters went in again, fancying he heard raspy breathing from Tomeroy. But the old man looked unchanged, unless—was there the faintest hint of blueness about his lips?

Masters shivered and turned away. Straight murder was bad enough; yet he himself had become more or less used to it in the course of his profession. This stealthy horror that crept up on a man, filling his veins and arteries, smothering him—it was too dreadful to contemplate.

Now, as the time dragged on, he set himself to a minute examination of the premises, then finally the yard and the street where the brougham had been, and where he had seen the three Chinese.

He managed to put in almost all of the waning afternoon in this fashion, but results were nil.

All the time he worked, Masters kept an ear cocked toward the house. There would come a commotion... the time was nearly up now. Would Tomeroy show the same symptoms? Shakily enough Masters took out a packet of cigarettes, lighted one, and inhaled deeply.

That instant it came. Through one of the casement windows Masters saw two or three men leap into sudden activity. There came shouts of excitement, almost of terror.

Masters ran for the door, burst into the living room, and there stopped stock still, his heart sinking into despair.

There on the rug, with the doctor and two policemen trying in vain to help him in the extremity of his suffocating agony, lay Josiah Tomeroy, white froth gathered in the corners of his mouth! His face was congested, bluish-yellow!

Even as Masters dropped to one knee, instinctively offering to do something, anything to help, the end came in one terrible convulsion.

"No use—that is all—you had it right!" choked the doctor, catching Masters' horrified glance. "But what *is* it? Do you know?"

"Fungus! Seaweed, perhaps! Oh—" and Masters rose to his feet, seizing the forearm of Gildersleeve. "We don't know much yet for sure. But I'm going back to Marriott's now. And as God is my judge, I'm going to catch the fiends who did this awful thing!"

"Stuffed men!" breathed the awed Gildersleeve. "*Stuffed men!*"

6

WRATH OF THE TAO TONG

ON THE RETURN journey Masters and his chauffeur ate at a lunch wagon. Just as they seated themselves Gildersleeve came in. The assistant had followed in his Ford. When they had finished a meager sort of meal, Masters sent Mitsui home with the big car, and accompanied Gildersleeve to the Marriott house at Pryde Estates.

The place was a humming hive of activity. Two big insurance companies had sent investigators; and these had a right to be satisfied.

Masters met Burton Marriott, only son of the dead Ralph Marriott. The younger man had come by plane from Cleveland. He seemed quiet and serious, aghast at the tragedy but still competent to take hold and manage.

Masters was glad to shift the care of the bereaved Mrs. Marriott and the soured spinster sister to his shoulders. The son immediately took them and Mrs. Marriott's maid in to the Ambassador Hotel in New York City, where they could have a day of rest before the funeral.

Cortelyou came from Mineola, bringing the latest news in respect to the saffron horror.

"We've studied the slides and microscopic specimens," he said tiredly. "That yellow stuff is fungus, all right—

though it's no known North American variety. Grows with terrific speed. Why, where we made those necessary incisions in the cadaver, nauseous bouquets of the stuff are growing! I've sent specimens to Jim Hall, Department of Biology, University of Columbia, to see if he can identify the fungus for us tomorrow morning. Now I'm going to sign off, and go home."

"We'll be doing the same in a couple of hours," nodded Masters. "That session at Scarsdale has done me up."

Lieutenant Connor was waiting for him then, however. Masters related briefly what had happened to Josiah Tomeroy.

"There are Chinese back of it," he concluded. "For some reason we don't know as yet, they are out to smash all the Ming relics they can find, it seems. Maybe some sort of political jealousy. Though why they'd have to do murder of innocent Americans is beyond me."

At that moment a policeman came in, motioning to Masters.

"Your Jap boy is outside. I think he's hurt, though I don't get his lingo any too damn well."

"Good Lord!" breathed the detective, starting for the door. "He wanted to get back to my place, because he hadn't finished the housework. Oh, there he is. What's wrong, Mitsui?"

The little yellow man was standing with one foot on the running board of the big car. His trouser leg was rolled up, showing a wiry shin and calf.

Now the Jap's swarthy countenance expressed anger and withering contempt in equal portions. His thin-lipped

mouth curved downward at the corners and his black eyes
sparkled like oil-polished onyx.

"I go back," he snapped, meaning that he had returned
to Masters' house. "Sneaky China boy theah. I tly catch.
No catch. Damn t'ief. Hit me with pokeh. No can stan' up."

He yanked up the leg of his trousers still further, and
showed a bruise on the right shinbone which must have
been agonizing and temporarily paralyzing.

"I fin' letteh. Fo' you."

Masters took the sealed envelope, holding it carefully by
the edges. It was addressed to "Mr. Masters," and the letters
forming those words had been cut out from eighteen-point
subheads on some tabloid paper. They were pasted on to
the cheap, pale pink envelope.

Before opening the epistle the detective dusted for
fingerprints. He found none—save Mitsui's, which were
familiar.

Carefully slitting the envelope then, he discovered a thin,
irregularly torn off rectangle of green paper, on which were
two marks of glossy black ink. The paper was the same kind
that Chino laundrymen buy in rolls and tear off for laundry
slips. The ink was the sort they apply with brushes.

Masters realized, frowning down at the slip, that one of
the two marks, which looked a trifle like a silhouette of an
octopus with the cramps, doubtless was a terse ideograph
message. The second figure, more carefully drawn, could
be a signature. It was a recognizable depiction of a rising
sun, with black lines angling upward to represent light rays.

On impulse, Masters went back to where Mitsui waited.

"Do you know what this means, Mitsui?" he asked, holding out the slip.

A twin to the cobra was there, wearing one of the yellow bands.

The little yellow man bent forward, then straightened with a jeering grin. "Yah!" he derided. "Japanese army fin' those allatime in Manchukuo. It mean, 'Go on some mo' an' you die!' Jus' mistake. *They* go on, but *China boy* die!"

Masters nodded grimly. "And this second mark?" he demanded. Things were looking up when his unknown adversaries would try to warn him off a case. But was this the actual name of a criminal society? Were those three Chinese who had murdered Tomeroy members of this society?

Mitsui scowled over the rising sun, and finally surmised it was the name of somebody who got up early in the morning.

"Figuring me the worm, eh?" said Masters dryly. "No, that isn't good enough. Wait. I'll get Gildersleeve. I believe there's a Chinese laundry right in Mineola where they do their ironing in the evening. We'll go there and ask."

AT CHARLIE MOY'S establishment in Mineola, Masters went in alone. Inside the steamy, rectangular room six black-aproned Celestials were wielding electric irons. In front, behind a short counter, sat fat Charlie Moy, hands folded over his second or third stomach.

Masters held the slip in front of him. "I'm just asking information," he said evenly. "Can you tell me just what this figure means?" He pointed at the black ideograph. "And then this rising sun signature?" He dropped his finger to the second drawing.

The result was amazing. The fat, torpid Chinaman, aroused no doubt from dreaming of a wealthy old age in the land of his birth, straightened, blanching to the color of cold bacon grease. His black eyes boggled. He opened blubbery lips, and a succession of squeaky screams issued. He padded up from the stool, tipping it over. He dashed back into the shop, waving fat arms, and paying no attention to the puzzled detective, who followed, demanding an explanation.

All of the ironers looked up, then at each other. With one accord they left their boards, grabbed for black cotton or mohair jackets, and dashed for the street, jabbering and squeaking their frightened singsongs!

Masters let them go. Not so Gildersleeve on the sidewalk! He folded arms around Charlie Moy—arms that would have held a man five times as strong as the fat Chinaman. Then Charlie Moy returned to his laundry, irrespective of desires which seemed to put many safe miles between himself and that terrible slip of paper.

Charlie Moy fairly groveled. Yes, he would tell—but he feared that dread signature and that warning message more than anything the white man's law could do to him.

Masters did his best to reassure. The message had been sent to another man, and had nothing to do with Charlie or his laundry. Now, just what did it mean?

In time, finding that he was not going to be let go until he spoke, Charlie gave the information. The black ideograph was a warning; the meaning was just as Mitsui had said. Someone was warned to stop what he was doing, on pain of death. Of course Charlie, half asleep when he had first seen it, had thought that meant shutting up his laundry.

"All right. Then, the signature—if that's what it is." Masters pointed at the setting sun with its rays of light angling upward.

"The Illustrious Society of Executioners!" groaned the terrified Celestial. "Oh, do not say that that honored name passed my lips!" he begged.

Masters pursed his lips in a low whistle. He let the Chinaman go, and walked out to the car with Gildersleeve.

"The Illustrious Society of Executioners!" he repeated in an awed voice. "In this country they *must* be the same as the Society of Fictile Artisans—known sometimes as the Tao Tong! That's a gang even the Hip Sings are afraid of! Why, the word Tao has two meanings—'reason,' and 'fictile.' Here it must be taken as 'fictile'—and then our hook-up with those three devils who killed Tomeroy is complete!"

He got into the car with Gildersleeve and told Mitsui to drive to his own place.

"Well," almost snored Gildersleeve, when he settled back

against the cushions, "an' what the hell, may I ask, does 'fictile' mean—in American?"

"Having to do with molding plastic materials, precious stuff like those Ming porcelains! Do you begin to see?"

"Huh! You mean these fellas make some other kinda crockery, an' are jealous of the Ming Company?" hazarded Gil.

"Oh, go back to sleep!" chuckled Masters. "The Mings passed into history some three hundred years ago. They weren't a manufacturing company, but a dynasty."

THE INSTANT MASTERS passed from the cool night air to the stuffy hotness of his closed cottage, he halted, grasping the sleepy assistant by the left arm.

Gil immediately straightened to the alert, staring about the dark hallway.

"Somebody's been in here," whispered Masters, his lips within an inch of the chunky man's ear. "Have your gun ready...."

He drew his own weapon, then reached left-handedly for the light switch. A cluster of wall lamps blazed. There was no one in sight.

Silently the pair tiptoed into the library, then across to the big room fitted up as a laboratory, and on further to the kitchen, each of the three bedchambers and the two baths.

There was no sign of an intruder anywhere. When Jigger Masters finished examining all the double-locked windows, the back door, and even the loft-attic (reached by a ladder and trap in one of the bedrooms) he shook his head puzzledly.

"I smelled something strange when I first came in. Don't

you get it, Gil? A faint but disagreeable smell that rather makes the hair stand up on the back of your neck?"

"Ask Mitsui. Mebbe he can smell," answered Gildersleeve. "My nose got all petro-morted when I worked in the garage. It don't begin to register on anything milder than a gin-and-garlic breath. But everything was locked tight. I don't think anybody was in. Mebbe some sewer gas…."

But the little yellow man detected the faint stench immediately. He went straightway to the electric refrigerator. The interior of this was too cold, if anything; nothing had spoiled. Mitsui walked around, head on one side, sniffing. At last, however, he was forced to give up. Both he and Masters felt instinctively that this odor was one of danger, though they could not place it.

As a last precaution the detective took the caged canary, Whistle It, and set him free. He flew about the house everywhere for ten minutes, alighting on the floor, on Jigger's shoulder, on the kitchen cabinet; and he showed no sign of anything except delight at the chance to stretch his wings.

"No gas, anyhow," said Masters then. "And so to bed. Wake me at seven, Mitsui, if I'm not up. See that the screens are locked, if you're leaving the windows open now."

Masters placed his pistol on the chiffonier, and doffed jacket, holster sling, tie and shirt. Then he sat down on the side of the single bed, to take off his shoes.

Two seconds later he suddenly froze. His oxford shoe dropped with a thump to the rug. Then he slowly, cautiously turned his head and started down with his left hand toward a slight ridge in the bedspread next to his thigh. The ridge moved slightly!

"Gil! Mitsui!" he shouted with all the power of his lungs.

"Don't go to bed! Come here, quick!" And he dashed out, to make sure that his emergency commands were obeyed. He caught both subordinates half-unclothed, but neither had as yet got under the covers.

They followed him wonderingly, and saw him dash into the laboratory, returning to his own bedchamber with a long glass rod and one of the dagger-stoppered bottles in which all the poisonous chemicals were kept. A skull and crossbones label on this particular brown glass bottle showed the symbol KCN, potassium cyanide.

With great caution then Masters raised the spread, single blanket and upper sheet from his bed. And as Gildersleeve saw what was revealed there, a gasping curse burst from his throat. "A snake!" he added. "Lord, an' it's got a *collar* on!"

Raising up one-third of its length from the linen sheet was a small but malignantly beautiful serpent. It was no more than thirty inches long; but the whitish bosom was striped horizontally with black, and the body glistened. Its neck or hood was puffing out now, and in the rear could be seen the telltale "spectacles"—the greenish-yellow markings of the cobra.

Masters' face was grim. He unstopped the poison bottle, dipped the glass rod, then with extreme caution advanced the moistened tip in the direction of the snake.

There came one quick strike... another! The serpent's fixed fangs in the upper jaw clicked against the end of the glass rod, and brownish squirts of deadly venom went to the bedsheet.

But the darting red tongue had encountered a clear drop of cyanide on the glass. And that was enough. Two seconds more, three, and then suddenly the erect head and neck of the cobra fell. It writhed, its puffed-out hood deflating. Then, more quickly than any mechanical injury could have made it happen, the snake lay motionless, quite dead.

"Better look right away in your own beds, men," advised Masters. "Take care, though! One of these fellows can kill a strong man in less than ten minutes!"

A yell from Gildersleeve brought him on the run, just when he had cut through the cobra's neck, and slipped off the curious metal band which the assistant had termed a collar. Waiting for the examination of this, Masters hastened in with the poison bottle.

A twin to the dead cobra was there, also wearing one of the yellow bands or collars. While Gildersleeve, his face for once showing not a sign of ruddy color, watched, cursing below his breath, Masters dispatched the second snake.

The third and last of the intruders was not in Mitsui's bed. It had escaped, and taken refuge in the clothespress of that room. They found it coiled around the upright wooden arm of a shoetree set in a pair of Mitsui's patent leather slippers.

When that was dead also, they carried the three bodies gingerly by the tails, and placed them on a newspaper on the floor of the living room. Masters cut off the two other collars, and handed them to his helpers.

"A trifle large for Mitsui, but a nice engraved gold thumb ring for you, Gil," he said dryly. "Do you see the delicately chased figure—the signet, if you want to call it that? Which, gentlemen, is a setting sun I believe all of us are going to remember. I hope that we can make it the *final* sunset of the terrible Tao Tong!"

7

PRISONER OF THE WART

JIGGER MASTERS LOOKED up from his coffee at the still sleepy assistant.

"I dreamt all four hours about snakes," said Gildersleeve grumpily, and noisily drank half a cup of scalding coffee.

"There is a message from Marsh Vandervoort. He got back last night from Massachusetts. I'm going in town to the Yancey Galleries, but that place doesn't open till ten. We'll stop at Marsh's mansion. There may be something indicated there for you to do while I'm in town. Meanwhile our problem:

"Here is a tong, a gang of Chinese robbers and murderers, who surely know the immense value of antique porcelains. They ruthlessly go after some of the finest known specimens, break in, kill—and incidentally kill another man who was associated with the treasures, though he had none in his possession—*but do not steal!* What is their object in doing that? We must search for that motive, because it *must* be the mainspring of everything!

"Then the secondary mystery, one I believe I can solve before the day is out. How were these deadly fungi implanted in the victims, neither of whom showed the slightest scratch or puncture of the skin?"

"Couldn't they swallow 'em—drink 'em in water like you take yeast?"

"No, there's no trace in the stom—" Masters stopped abruptly. He straightened, and the flash of an inspiration showed in his craggy features. "Zoöspores, by Heaven!" he cried, leaping to his feet. "Gil, you've presented me with a part of the solution!" With that he strode into the living room, where on shelves to the ceiling were the greater number of his reference books.

Gildersleeve looked after him, grinning dubiously. "I'm good, I think," he announced, pouring a final cup of coffee. "Only I wish somebody'd explain it to me!"

The only explanation he received that morning, however, was one Masters vouchsafed after brief but meaty phone conversations with James Hail, professor of biology at Columbia, and Dr. Cortelyou, medical examiner for Nassau County. Masters and Gildersleeve got in the car and were being driven by Mitsui over to Biskra Harbor, where Marsh Vandervoort and his bride lived.

"How it was done I still have only a faint idea," said Masters, breaking his jubilant silence. "But the actual means employed to kill these men—and stuff them— seems plain. They were murdered by vegetables, that swim!"

DOROTHY VANDERVOORT CAME, gayly clad and stepping lightly with the sheer joy of youth and love that was in her, but with a distinct shadow of foreboding over her pretty face.

"Mr. Masters, and Mr. Gildersleeve," she greeted. "I— oh, you don't want Marsh to go out on this awful crime, do you?" she asked immediately, distress in her voice. "It—it scares me. I saw that dead man up at the morgue. The Japanese. He was—was—" She shuddered.

"Never fear, little lady," smiled Masters. "I just want a few words with Marsh, and then you can take him to Lake George or somewhere. I'll be glad to have you two safely out of this grim business."

They entered the big stone house which was still known as Corlaes Manor; and a few moments later Marshall Vandervoort came, attired in pyjamas and blue-brocaded lounging robe. His face was rueful.

"What a hell of a helper I turned out to be!" he said, with a comical gesture of resignation. "It's a gorgeous case, Jigger, and I'd give a lot of money to follow through with you. But Dot says she'll make me a widower—grass variety—if I do, before *I* succeed in leaving her a widow. So we're going down to Forest Hills for a week of outdoor pingpong."

Masters said nothing at all about the three cobras, or about the natatory vegetables he suspected of killing and stuffing three victims.

The young millionaire had followed the death of Ichiara Kagodi, and had seen the police and the coroner up at Westboro, Massachusetts. There was such a complete similarity between the case and that of both other victims of the deadly yellow fungus, however, that Masters found nothing added to his knowledge. The Jap had been killed in exactly the same way; and there was no sign of a hypodermic puncture. Of course the fall from a plane had damaged his body so greatly that this was less certain than in the cases of Marriott and Josiah Tomeroy; but the Massachusetts authorities were stumped. They had decided to hold and then adjourn their inquest pending more information from Mineola.

One item of information changed Masters' plans for the day, however. On returning to Long Island at nine the previous night, Marsh had called up Devereaux Yancey, the proprietor of the galleries on Forty-fourth Street, at the art dealer's Locust Valley residence.

"I know Dev pretty well," said Marsh. "He's a good soul, but a regular Caspar Milquetoast when it comes to anything outside his own profession. So timid about anything like violence or physical contact that a ride in the subway in rush hour makes him ill for a week.

"I wanted to know all about Ichiara and those porcelains, and so told him there were these mysterious deaths connected with them. That scared him so he could scarcely talk at all. But in the end I did learn something. He's not going to New York today at all—leaving the shop in the hands of his employees, and asking a police guard for the galleries, and also one for his home out here. I don't suppose he's in any real danger."

"Has he any more of those porcelains?" demanded Masters.

"No; not a one that I know of. His private specialty is etching. The galleries, of course, are sold out clean on Ming porcelain, and probably never will handle any more."

"Then I think there is no danger," said Masters. "What was it you learned?"

"Oh—well, just about one contact of this fellow Ichiara Kagodi. There seems to be next to nothing known of him. Dev tried to find out all he could, you know, before he consented to buy that Ming collection. No success. Ichiara just grinned at him and kept his own counsel.

"But Dev did see him two or three times with an older man—and that man already had aroused Dev's curiosity. He is a funny old duffer, wears a red wig, and uses a crutch. At least Dev is pretty sure it's a red wig.

"Before Dev Yancey had ever set eyes on the Jap, this old codger, who called himself Jones, had been in the galleries a number of times. He talked about Chinese art, and then surprised Dev almost into a spasm by admiring and actually buying a seventeenth century enameled copper plate!

"You see, Dev had sized up the old fellow as being chatty but poor. When he actually hauled out a wallet and paid three hundred dollars in cash for that plate, Dev was astounded. Just had the thing wrapped up carefully, and hobbled out with it under his arm! Never even left an address.

"But he came again. Several times, in fact. He bought a Siwen-te jug—one dated 1431 A.D. in terms of our calendar. Another time he picked up a Ch'ien Lun snuff jar. Then one day, after he had asked repeatedly about porcelains, Dev showed him a real treasure. It was a Sung Dynasty image of the war god, Kwan-ti, in porcelain, and valued by Dev at $4000.

"Old Jones positively beamed. He handled it lovingly, then pulled out a bill case and planked down four one-thousand-dollar bills! 'I'll take it right along with me,' he cackled, happy as could be.

"When the old man left with his heavy parcel—using the crutch, you know—Dev followed him. The old man only walked about a block or two. He'd refused even to let Dev or a clerk carry the parcel to his train for him. He went to the corner of Vanderbilt, next to the Grand Central Station, and waited there near the corner. In about five minutes a Packard limousine with a liveried chauffeur drove up and picked him up.

"Dev did do one thing—get the number of the car's plates. But then he didn't follow it up right away. You see, Dev is timid. He got to thinking that maybe old Jones just wore his wig and shabby clothes when he went shopping, so the prices wouldn't be jacked up too high. As long as his money wasn't counterfeit, Dev had no right to snoop.

"There never were any more sales. The old duffer came several times more, but didn't seem to find anything that suited. Twice then Dev saw him talking with the Jap, who later identified himself as Ichiara. Dev got the notion they met there by appointment. They separated and pretended to be strangers when Dev came near.

"Then later, after Ichiara was trying to sell the Mings to Dev, he saw the Jap and old Red-wig Jones having luncheon together. That was what really persuaded Dev to plunge for the porcelains, as he thought he could sell some of them, anyhow, to Jones.

"But after the sale he never set eyes on Jones again! It was lucky that Marriott and Josiah Tomeroy came along when he advertised that auction, or else Dev might have had a lot of capital tied up for years.

"When he decided on the auction, and was having the announcements engraved, Dev remembered the car plate number he had jotted down. Of course he looked it up then, and sent one of the announcements to the man he had known as Jones. Of course that was not his name at all. You'll be interested now, Jigger!

"That old codger, who seemed to have developed such a yen for Chinese art in his declining years, was none other than the famous Seth Bryson, of Hempstead! The recluse who owns that world-notorious freak house over there on Cathedral Avenue—"

"The Brick Wart!" ejaculated Masters in real surprise.

"Well, at least that Packard limousine was licensed in his name," corroborated Marsh with a grin. "He's the rich old geezer who used to manufacture bricks, isn't he?"

"Yes. Hm." The detective's mind was racing, the expression of his hazel eyes abstracted. "For ten years they say he's never appeared in public—just stayed shut up in that weird place. Never allowed any visitors at all. Well," and Masters straightened with decision, "he's going to have visitors right now, today. Come on, Gil!"

THE FOUR-MILE TRIP, with Mitsui driving, occupied only a few minutes. During this time Masters ignored a question or two fired in his direction. Gildersleeve, recognizing the signs, philosophically applied himself to his pipe.

The Bryson home was renowned as a freak. Though the plot of ground enclosed by the solid eight-foot brick walls was fully half an acre, and fronted one of the loveliest streets in the mid-island part of Nassau, there was not a shrub, not even a blade of grass, inside the walls.

There was no ivy on the strangely curving walls of the house. The brick in the courtyard, and the brick of the house itself, was chiefly a cream-white, fine-textured front-brick made under heavy pressure from white clay.

There was a slender line of scarlet used for trim on the house.

There in the midst of the barren yard stood a white stag of solid iron; and a coterie of little, bearded gnomes played bowls like the men of Henrik Hudson. The house raised itself like a bubble, puffed up out of boiling syrup.

There was not an angle, not a straight line on the exterior. Instead of rising sheer, the brick floor of the yard suddenly slanted up more and more sharply, not reaching vertical until the ceiling line of the first floor was attained.

A convex second story was topped at last by a sort of mushroom third floor.

There was no visible front door, no back door, no door at all. A spiral way, like unto that built around the ascending Tower of Babel, led around and to the roof, by means of a sort of trapdoor of brick, counterweighted. This was kept closed.

The actual doors and windows were finished in brick shutters on the outside. When they all were closed, the Wart for all practical purposes was hermetically sealed. Presumably it had a modern ventilating and air conditioning system, else its inhabitants must have smothered.

"This is an odd number for sure," said Masters as they drew up opposite the massive bronze gate which gave upon Cathedral Avenue. "If anything goes wrong, phone Connor—and let him explain to the police of Hempstead. They may look sourly enough on me as an intruder, but I mean to see Bryson one way or another. They say there are four or five other people beside the brick manufacturer who live there. And we know now that he has a car and chauffeur.

"Think this over—it may prove important. There is no gate or driveway for a car in that eight-foot wall! Does Bryson keep it in some public garage, and have the chauffeur call for it there?"

Masters crossed the broad avenue, the terrace and sidewalk, and stopped before the wrought-bronze door. Here in the wall was a recess, holding a pearl button. Masters pressed this and waited. Three minutes, five minutes passed. Then more impatiently he pressed again.

Then sounded a sharp *click*. A rectangular panel some eight by four inches had opened in the bronze door. In the aperture was framed the stern, forbidding visage of a man of middle age, lean, clean-shaven, and with skin of a grayish undertint tightly drawn across protuberant cheekbones. A peculiar squint or slant of the eyes suggested sullenness, cruelty.

"No callers are allowed. Why did you ring?" the man inside rasped. There was no pretense of civility in his manner.

"Tell Seth Bryson I'm here because of the Ming porcelain," snapped Masters, certain that nothing less than a shock would get him the interest of this scowling servitor. "I think it's a matter of life and death—to Bryson!"

The man at the hole in the door did not answer. His narrow eyes grew rounder, and his face drew closer to that of Masters. The detective smelled a curiously aromatic breath, not offensive but strange. A little bit like medicinal aloes.

"Those porcelains are always life and death—to Bryson," answered the guardian of the door in an ominous tone. "You can wait."

Then suddenly the panel in the door slid closed with a click. But Masters was ready for just that. He had dropped a copper cent in the groove. Now the panel failed by a quarter inch to close. The servitor did not notice.

GIVING THE MAN five seconds, Masters then opened a jackknife, inserting the heavy blade in the crack between the bronze panel and its frame. When completely closed, it was locked; but now there was no difficulty in sliding it back an inch or two more, against the push of a moderate spring.

Thus, crouching a little, the detective peered inside the grounds of the Wart, and watched a gawky, tall figure in a tail coat stride back to the house.

Whether or not Bryson would be sufficiently impressed by that curt message, so that he would consent to see a visitor, only time would tell. Masters settled to wait, getting a good picture of this queer establishment as the servant walked toward the slanting spiral entranceway.

The black-coated man walked jerkily. But that did not explain what he suddenly did. Just before he reached the slant which led to the spiral upward way, he gathered himself and leaped across a space of open yard which in no way differed in externals from the rest. Then he went on just as before.

"Now, why did he do that? Burglar alarm, d'you suppose?" conjectured the watching detective.

From the gate, because of the bulge of the second story and the overhanging eaves above, Masters could not see the tiled roof of the Brick Wart. But across on the other side of Cathedral Avenue waited the Studebaker with Mitsui at the wheel. Gildersleeve stood on the running board and stared. From this position he could see over the eight-foot wall, with its defense of broken bottles set in concrete, and get a plain view of the second story and mushroom roof. This tiled canopy, of course, covered what there was of the third floor.

Of a sudden he emitted a suppressed sound which might have been a curse of surprise. Then—

"Can you c'mere a second, Jigger?" he called across the street, voice tense. "I see somep'n damn funny...."

Masters turned and sprinted back to the car. There he swung about, following the excited assistant's pointing finger. And in spite of himself he cried out in surprise.

Near the very top of the tiled mushroom a small door or window had swung open. The aperture could not be more than ten inches or a foot square; and the thickness of the tiles which swung out made it appear like the door of a fireproof wall safe.

From this small, square hole projected a slender, bare arm. And the hand waved something small and white— surely, from its size, this could be nothing but a woman's cambric or lace handkerchief.

Then for a fugitive instant a face appeared. From this distance neither Masters nor the burly Gildersleeve could tell much about the face, except that it was feminine. Gil cursed softly, wonderingly below his breath, while Masters watched in rigid silence. What possible connection could such a phenomenon have with the mystery of the stuffed men?

With a suddenness that suggested violence up there inside the room concealed by that odd-shaped roof the face and arm disappeared. Then the small, thick door swung closed. From outside it was impossible to discern any crack or other sign of jointure.

"Get Connor and the Hempstead police," directed Masters quietly, "I'm going in there—and it doesn't look much like an invitation, now. There's a woman captive up there!"

"Oh, hell, let me come along with you, chief!" pleaded Gildersleeve. "I hate to—"

But Jigger Masters rarely repeated commands. He walked rapidly across the street, and took up his position at the gate. Through the slit at one side of the sliding panel he was just in time to see the manner in which the black-coated servant emerged from the interior of the Wart.

At a height from the ground along the slanting upward spiral way which corresponded with the first floor above an English basement, a large door swung ponderously open. This too, like the square, small window high above, was camouflaged with an outside covering of creamy white brick, across which ran a line of the scarlet trim.

Behind him he heard his car start up with a rush. That was good. There might be no end of trouble here, particularly if the Hempstead police were not forewarned; but Gil could be counted on to take care of that.

The lanky servant descended the spiral way, and the hidden door closed slowly behind him. Masters noted with interest that now when the man reached the expanse of brick on the floor of the yard, he made no effort to jump. If that had been some queer contrivance like an alarm to warn the Wart-dwellers of skulkers, it now probably was turned off.

OUT TO THE gate came the servitor. His gaunt, Tartar

countenance was gloomier than ever, if possible. He spoke not a syllable until he reached the gate, threw aside the metal panel, and brought his disagreeable countenance so close to that of the visitor that Masters again could smell that peculiar aromatic odor. Then in a funereal voice:

"Mr. Bryson is indisposed and cannot receive anyone today. Perhaps if you would write out your name and the precise nature of your business—" He held up a small pad, to which a pencil was attached by a brass-link chain.

Masters moved like a flash. Grasping the wrist, instead of the proffered pad, he yanked the coated arm through the aperture clear to the shoulder, clamping it with the elbow bent so the other man was helpless.

"I'm not an enemy—yet," said Masters briefly. "But I can act like one if it's necessary. Unlock the door!"

One blasting oath, then a string of words in a language utterly foreign to Masters, burst from the man in the black coat. For a few seconds he tried to struggle; but the pain from his clamped arm stopped this.

"All right. I'll open it. But where the hell d'you think you'll be when you do get in?"

Masters allowed him a little freedom of movement, keeping sharp watch as the other reached an arm over to a ponderous lever. There sounded a click of an opening lock, and the heavy door swung inward.

Following the heavy weight with his body, until there was a space of two feet, the detective suddenly let go his captive's arm and stepped inside. He caught the edge of the door with his left hand and shoved it closed. Right hand flashed to the butt of his pistol in the armpit sling, and he waited.

With a gritted sound of anger the black-coated man slowly let drop one of the tails of his coat, and raised his hands shoulder high. He had decided against chancing his luck against that fast lapel draw.

"Turn around," bade Jigger briskly.

The man obeyed. Reaching under the coat tails, the detective brought up an ugly six-inch weapon, a bulldog derringer, double-barreled and of some immense caliber. Probably a .56, one of the largest ever sold in America, Masters surmised. A devastating firearm at a few paces, though inaccurate.

"Now we'll go in and see Bryson," said Jigger calmly, dropping the loaded derringer in his jacket pocket, and disregarding the answering snarl from the captive. "I've sent for the Hempstead police. If any harm has come to that young woman, we'll just about take Bryson and you apart."

This brought up the swarthy servitor. "Woman?" he queried, wrinkling his brows until the back smudges of hair met in the center of his forehead. "What t'hell woman you talking about? There isn't any woman here—no female except possibly Miss Lois. And I thought she was out somewhere."

"It's Miss Lois I mean. Who is she?"

"Oh, she's Mr. Bryson's granddaughter. What do you want of her?" In spite of surliness, the man seemed frank enough now.

"Lead on," bade Masters, giving him a push toward the spiral way. "I want to see Bryson and Miss Lois—if she happens to be the girl you've got imprisoned up there in that top room."

"Imprisoned?" The trap mouth gaped with what seemed genuine amazement and alarm. "There ain't a soul shut up—except we all have to stay inside the walls out there. Look here. It won't do you a damn bit of good to get in that door. Old Bryson won't let anybody see him. He's scairt of something. If I open that door, I'll just about get canned. And my wife, too. Jobs even now aren't too easy to get."

"I'm going to see Bryson," Masters said sternly. "However, I'll tell him I made you open up. What is your name?"

"Marfowski," he snarled. "Bryson calls me Murphy. There ain't anybody looking for me, so don't think I give a damn!"

At the click of the lock, the un-Celtic Murphy pressed inward. The heavy door swung smoothly, revealing an arched hallway tiled underfoot in a mosaic pattern. Indirect daylight-lighting came from hidden blue nitrogen bulbs studded along the arched ceiling.

Masters then and later wondered grimly to himself what the electric light bill for this house could be. Every room was lighted twenty-four hours a day by electricity, except when one of the inmates had reason to snap off the current in order to sleep. Most of the time no windows or doors were open to the outside.

Sullenly, though evidently feeling that affairs had passed out of his hands now, the guide opened the first door on his left, and walked on in as Masters motioned him to precede.

This was a richly furnished but tasteful drawing room. The room was about twenty-five feet in width by thirty in length. Murphy went straight on down to the end wall, and pressed a concealed button. An oblong panel clicked open, showing what was evidently a microphone speaker.

"This is the only way I ever get to talk with him, unless he sends for me," explained Murphy. He pressed a button beside the microphone, and then spoke in a slightly raised voice.

"It's that gentleman who was outside, Mr. Bryson. He used—tactics on me, and got in. He has a gun. Two of them now. He says that there is a girl or woman imprisoned up in the storeroom on the top floor, and that he has sent for the police. He wants to see her, and to have a talk with you. Will you admit him?"

THE BLANK SILENCE was disturbing. Murphy stared at a rectangular, empty space of wall, then up to a higher spot. A loud speaker or announcer was probably set there. But if so, it remained silent.

Murphy went back, touched the button three times, and then spoke again: "Mr. Bryson! Are you there?"

No answer. Murphy turned around toward the waiting detective. "I'm sorry, sir," he said, frowning a little. "Mr. Bryson sometimes goes up to the third floor, and sometimes he is in the basement. He has a laboratory there, I've heard."

"You've heard?" repeated Masters. "Haven't you been all around this house yourself?"

"No, sir. I live on this floor. My room is on the other side of the hall. All on this side belong to Mr. Bryson. They are protected by locks, alarms, and other devices. Nobody at all can get in, unless Mr. Bryson admits that person."

"Who cleans and makes the beds?"

"I do, with the help of Miss Lois. Mr. Bryson lets her or

me into one room at a time; and while we're there we can't get out. Then for lunch and dinner, I bring those meals on a tea wagon, to Miss Lois, out there in the hall. On the stroke of one o'clock and seven, she is admitted to the little room where Mr. Bryson eats. She eats those two meals with him, and brings out the tea wagon for me."

"All right. The other servants? I suppose there are some more?" asked Masters.

"Of course. Cook and assistant cook—though why they need two, I don't know. They're on vacation now. That's all of us." Murphy showed signs of nervousness, glancing over his shoulder at the microphone.

"Chauffeur?" persisted Masters.

"No, of course not. Mr. Bryson does not keep a car."

Masters did not show by any sign that he knew better. "Where does Miss Lois Bryson sleep?" he asked.

"On the second floor. She used to care for old Mrs. Bryson before her death. But it is not Miss Bryson, sir. Her name is Miss Lois Ingalls. She is Mr. Bryson's granddaughter; an orphan, I believe."

"I see." Masters glanced up the stairway. "Well, try and get in touch again with Bryson. It would pay him, I think, to talk to me before the police get here. For myself, I'm going upstairs—and I *don't* want you to follow! Can I reach the third floor by this staircase?"

"Well—the second floor. The third story is only a half-portion, sir. You go up by a central stair. You'll see it in the upstairs corridor. But that is always locked, up there. Mr. Bryson uses it as a gallery, and doesn't allow visitors."

"A gallery, you said?" repeated Masters softly. "Just what kind of a gallery? Pictures?"

"Oh, no, sir," replied Murphy, nervously. "His interests lie in another field entirely. He collects objects of art. Pottery, chiefly. Oriental art. That third-floor room contains hundreds of thousands of dollars worth of it. I don't suppose there is a collection to compare with it, anywhere in the United States!

"That's why I say you couldn't get in—and why there is no prisoner there. You will find Miss Lois somewhere on the second floor, if you call. Perhaps she could help you. But I'm sure that the third floor—"

But Masters paid no further attention to the nervously voluble butler. Noiselessly, hand on his pistol, the detective was ascending the staircase.

The butler, meanwhile, went over to the microphone and pressed the signal button.

"Mr. Bryson! Mr. Bryson!" he called again and again; but there came no answering voice.

Above his head and over at the side of the room, a small opening suddenly appeared. Though even Murphy guessed it not, this was a spy hole from which Seth Bryson was wont to look over any caller carefully before admitting him to one of the guarded inner rooms.

Now the black eye which looked down upon the butler was narrow—or slanted.

It was unwinking, baleful. It stared a full minute. Then it vanished. In its place came something round with a hole in its end. This affair was shellacked bamboo.

It depressed a little in the direction of Murphy. A thin, grayish stream suddenly issued from it! One would have had to stand very close to hear the faint rush of air which accompanied the grayish, vapor-like substance, which spread and diffused through the air directly above the butler's pate, descending so slowly that it might have been said to hang there like fog vapor in the branches of a tree. Death hanging in dead air....

Murphy did not see it at all—then or ever. He smelled it, however. Straightening after one of his fruitless calls, he sniffed, wrinkling his nose, and frowning.

"Now what the hell is *that?*" he muttered, sniffing again and again, and looking vacantly about the room. The peephole up at the side had closed. He saw nothing.

He sniffed around for fully fifteen minutes, but found no sign. Then he opened the door, and did his best to drive out the smell by fanning a sofa pillow in the air.

But slow, loathsome doom had set its seal upon him. Each of those fine particles in the air was an egg—of a certain kind. A vegetable's egg. An egg that had fine, tiny hairs called cilia, which acted like the fins of a fish, and let the egg-vegetable swim in a man's lungs… through his blood stream!

Serge Marfowski, known familiarly as Murphy, had been marked for death by the saffron horror!

8

BEHIND WHAT DOOR?

JIGGER MASTERS FELT the tingling impact of unseen eyes. Was the master of this mystery house one of the watchers?

"The law would acquit Bryson if he blew me off these stairs with buckshot!" reflected the detective grimly.

Pausing at the first landing to listen intently, Jigger then advanced slowly, noiselessly. His pistol was drawn. He kept his back to the outside wall. Back there in the living room he had quitted, Murphy's voice, low and insistent, came again, calling Bryson. Where could the owner be?

The second floor was chiefly an L-shaped hall, softly lighted, with blue and gold rugs and a little rattan furniture gayly upholstered. It was spectrally quiet. All the doors opening on the hall were closed. Masters tried the knob of one. It resisted his efforts.

SHRUGGING BRIEFLY, HE turned toward the elbow of the hall. Here was the staircase leading to the third-floor gallery. It was not conspicuous, and did not look as though it were much in use. Set back in a sort of shallow cabinet, it revealed itself as a spiral affair of black-painted iron, with a corrugated rubber stair carpet.

Above there was no light. Masters supposed there must be a door, probably locked.

Anyhow, it had been from up there, under the tiled roof, that the woman had signaled.

With a last moment of listening, hearing nothing at all from this second floor where Lois Ingalls was presumed to be, he turned to the iron stair and mounted it quickly.

The head of the iron stair ended in a cabinet not unlike a telephone booth, though slightly larger. There was one door straight ahead. It was cold to the touch—green enamel over steel, like the entrance of a safety deposit vault. There was no knob.

Over the keyhole was a metal mask, one in which there was no secrecy, however, as a quarter-circle arc where the paint had been scratched away revealed it instantly.

Jigger Masters held a fountain pen flashlight, examining the keyhole. This was no simple affair, but a modern key-combination with the keyholes staggered. Dropping to one knee, he placed his ear to the keyhole and listened. There was no sound—though it was doubtful if anything like an ordinary movement in the room or corridor beyond could have come to him through this blind aperture.

Taking a small, flat case resembling a doctor's hypodermic case from his pocket, Masters clicked it open. Inside was an array of delicate instruments. Some of these folded. Some had queer hooks and bends. There were four skeleton keys and two blanks. With this hand-made equipment and sufficient time, the man who had taught Jigger Masters all he knew about locks could enter doors thought to be thiefproof.

For several minutes then the detective was busy. He got

no less than four of his instruments into the keyhole, and ascertained the manner in which the flanges of a key actuated the tumblers.

Was there a strange shuffling, stirring sound within?

Masters started back, dropping one hand to the butt of his pistol as he stared in fascination at the green door.

"Open!" he suddenly cried, crouching a little, with left hand on the painted iron rail of the spiral staircase.

The cool iron quivered under his touch!

With a suppressed cry of astonishment he swung about, jamming the tools and case into his jacket pocket, and started down the spiral stair as fast as he could go.

He was too late! Now he had to scramble back to the cabinet outside the green door.

Sliding upward smoothly on its oiled uprights, the spiral stair had folded and risen. It now formed an impenetrable barrier of metal barring the mouth of the well leading down to the second floor.

"Glad they left me room to stand here!" he reflected grimly. He took out the tools again, and one of the key blanks.

"It's the locked door now," he thought, "no matter if the whole damned Tao Tong is waiting on the other side!"

9

THE NOSELESS MONSTERS

WITH DESPERATE CONCENTRATION he set himself to the task of key filing. He bore down heavily to minimize the rasping sounds. For minutes he worked steadily, taking measurements every two or three minutes with his delicate instruments.

Memory of the woman who had waved through a small window in this very attic which lay beyond the green enameled door made him swift. As far as he could judge, it was almost done now. Just a stroke of the file here and there, to polish off a few projections. And then would come the exasperating though fairly simple business of trying all the simple turns and re-turns which would make up the combination.

A tiny scratching sound at his feet caused him to start back, tense. A triangle of white—part of a piece of paper—had appeared at the bottom of the green-enameled door!

Revolver in hand now, and the tools and key blank set noiselessly to the floor, he stooped slowly, keeping his eyes and revolver trained on the door.

The paper came through the crack at the bottom of the door, though with difficulty. He stood up, holding it in his left hand, glancing at it—and not relaxing vigilance in the least. Someone was on the other side of that door.

One glance down at the oblong slip of paper, and his wide mouth set in a harsh line. It was the familiar laundry slip bearing the signature of the Tao Tong!

But this time there was something added. Just below the sinister setting sun was a tiny figure of an animal in silhouette. Masters stared, and an involuntary shiver ran through him. In a way this was a sort of honor, provided, of course, that they meant this message for him. He was sure they did....

The figure there just below the sun with its slanted rays was that of a whiskered rat!

Jigger did a most peculiar thing. His second hip pocket, balancing the set of miniature tools made for him by the burglar, held a small first aid case.

Now he opened this swiftly. Out of it he took an ounce phial of gummy collodion, a substance useful for sealing cuts temporarily, or for coating the ends of human fingers to prevent leaving the evidence of fingerprints. Though a freely flowing liquid, owing to its ether content, collodion dries in a few minutes when exposed to air. It forms a layer of artificial skin.

Near the roots of his wiry black hair at the crown of his head, the detective had another small phial hidden. This contained exactly ten drops of the same liquid once carried by the women of Russia's famous Battalion of Death, when going forth to do battle against bestial male enemies. But Jigger kept it hidden there as a last-ditch offensive weapon, ordinarily. Only once in his career had he been compelled to use it. That time he killed a degenerate who otherwise would have added another horror to his roster of sex crimes.

This time, oddly enough, the little phial of death would be a defensive weapon. Taking care to breathe none of the fumes from it, he emptied the ten drops into the collodion, and quickly shook up the mixture. The collodion would hold the more volatile substance. There would be no danger now—for him. Not from the drug.

The mysterious operation, which entailed a swift, partial undressing, was completed in less than two minutes. Then after a short wait for the collodion to set, the detective again adjusted his clothes. He took up the key, which now he hoped would open the door, just as soon as he could run through the simple permutations and combinations to be made with two or three turns this way and that.

But even as he picked up the crude key he had made from the blank, and was about to insert it in the keyhole, the act was arrested. On the other side of the door had sounded a faint shuffling.

HE CROUCHED, PISTOL ready. Then, although he heard no click of lock, the door of green enamel slowly started to open.

He watched it, fascinated, seeing no sign of an enemy in the slowly widening aperture, but conscious of a sickened premonition in the pit of his stomach. The detached thought came that this must be the way condemned criminals at Sing Sing feel, when being led from their death cells down the corridor toward that other narrow green door....

With one sudden leap he was inside, crouching, ready to fire at anyone, anything—and finding himself unexpectedly alone in a small, odd-shaped room, the outer wall of

which was the segment of a circle. Alone! He stared unbe-
lievingly about. The door had opened. Certainly there had
not been time for anyone to leave it, cross to one of the
two side doors of this chamber, and disappear. His eyes
were fastened on the green door. No one was near it. Still,
it moved!

At first slow, then increasing its acceleration to a sudden
slam, it went closed. The metallic click of the lock told
Jigger that now, unless his crude key fitted, and he found
the combination of turns, he had merely exchanged pris-
ons.

"The devil!" he breathed, darting glances back over his
own shoulders, expecting an attack which did not come.

The room was really a gallery, remotely similar to the
one at Ralph Marriott's in which he had kept his ceramics collection. This was evidently one of several galleries,
opening one into the other.

There was no trace of a window. Light, as everywhere in
the Wart, came indirectly from the blue bulbs of daylight
nitrogens. Three permanent shelves, unglassed, ran contin-
ually around the curved outside wall. On these shelves were
placed perhaps fifty specimens of foreign antique pottery.

Masters had seen specimens of such work in the Metropolitan. He thrilled momentarily at the realization that this
was pottery from ancient Greece, dating from about 700
B.C. up to the beginning of the Christian era!

Immediate peril, however, transcended any desire to
look at the possibly unique display.

Sure that his movements were closely observed, the
detective walked almost casually to the nearest door of
the two which led out of this chamber at the ends. There

was a knob here, and a big brass key stood out horizontally from the keyhole.

To his surprise, the door opened. Pausing only to pocket the key, Jigger Masters stepped through into a chamber identical in shape and similar in furnishings, a room also silent and empty of occupants. Here was Egyptian pottery, very ancient stuff.

Masters saw the plan of this attic floor now. There were probably eight rooms up here under the mushroom of tile roof. Each room constituted an eighth segment of a circle.

In the very next chamber breathless surprise awaited. When Masters attempted to turn the knob, the door resisted. The key was there, however, so with a tautening of the muscles and an increased alertness, he turned it. The lock made a rasping sound, followed by a dull click.

With one jerk he threw the door wide. Then he clutched the pistol, staring. Here was the woman who had signaled!

On a long central table lay a feminine figure, trussed with thin yellow rope in what must have been a torturing position. Lying on her back, the girl or woman—she looked to be tall and well formed, with a wealth of waved hair reddish brown in color, but skin chalk white with the pallor almost of death—had elbows bent down around the sides of the narrow table. Below this her wrists were corded together, a space of two feet separating the fingertips to prevent any possible self-help.

Tight ropes bound down her thighs cruelly, pressing through the light blue summer dress. And more ropes, knotted about each ankle, held these close together, with her heels just over the lower end of the table. One slipper had fallen to the rug, revealing a slender foot in silk stocking.

She was gagged, but not entirely unconscious. As Masters came into the room she moaned, and her breast rose and fell perceptibly. Her eyes remained closed.

He gave a suppressed exclamation of relief, and went immediately to her side. With his jackknife he swiftly cut the strong silk ropes, and drew out the gag. There were deep marks across her cheeks, and on her wrists, but she sighed in relief. He saw that she was young, probably no more than twenty-two or twenty-three, magnificently molded of figure, and of the milky complexion owned only by those fortunate women in whose hair lie some glints, at least, of auburn.

Looking about him now, listening, Masters heard nothing at all save some vague thumpings which seemed to come from somewhere below stairs.

"Hope that's Gil, back with Connor and the Hempstead police," he thought—then shrugged. How would they be able to get into the Brick Wart? Somehow right away he would have to locate the hidden window in the wall of this floor, the one from which this girl had signaled. Then a dropped message, perhaps....

HE LIFTED HER head, slipping one arm behind her shoulders, and brought her to a sitting position on the edge of the table beside him.

"Come, wake up!" he bade quietly but tensely. Never for an instant did he relax his careful watch. Was this a trap? Was this beautiful girl bait in the trap?

Jigger Masters was stirred. Even in the tense awareness of peril that pressed upon them both, he knew that even before this girl opened her eyes to look at him, she attracted him.

"Some time, under other circumstances, I'd like to meet a girl like this, just the same," he reflected with a certain grim wistfulness. Presently he was rewarded by a tremor of the long eyelashes and a deep sigh.

There came a dry gasp of terror, and the girl straightened, tensing and trying to free herself from his supporting embrace.

"Let *go* of me!" she screamed, fighting like a tigress.

Jigger instantly drew his arms away and stepped back from the table. The girl, blue eyes blazing with fright and resentment in which a tinge of bewilderment now was appearing, half crouched on the other side of the table from him.

"I'm sorry to frighten you," he said. "We're both locked in here by some kind of a gang. I found you unconscious. So I cut you loose and was trying to revive you." He gestured at the yellow silk ropes on the floor. "Are you Miss Ingalls?"

She nodded. "Oh-h!" The back of one hand rose to her mouth, as if she still could feel the gag. "You—where do you come from?"

He told her his name. Then, feeling this would reassure her far better than words, he reached into his jacket pocket and brought forth the double-barreled bulldog derringer he had taken from Murphy.

"If you know how to shoot, take this," he said. "It's loaded, and a touchy sort of weapon. But it will kill a man extremely dead, at short range—"

As she reached forward across the table and gingerly took the ugly little pistol from his hand, Jigger caught the veriest shade of movement or change on one of the bare shelves of this room. What was it? He swung about, but for a second could see nothing. It came strongly to mind just then, however, that instead of looking at heavily laden shelves of pottery of some sort, he saw only the bare wall and the spaces where lately there had been a considerable number of pieces of ceramic ware. This fact was evidenced by dust rings of varying size, showing here and there upon the natural-finished oak shelves.

But all speculation fled. He saw, just above one of the shelves, a tiny wicket in the wall open. Through this square aperture, no more than the size of two penny matchboxes set side by side, came then a tube of shellacked bamboo, with a round, dark hole in the end! It pushed out six inches into the room, and appeared to train on them!

Jigger Masters realized that here at last was a concrete evidence of the menace which sought his life, promising him in the last message the torture of the rat.

With a strangled cry he snatched his own heavy pistol from its armpit sling, and sent one thunderous shot directly at the small target of the aperture. Another!

As though snatched from behind the wall, the tube of bamboo suddenly disappeared. There was a single, minor wailing note that ebbed away, and with a click the square wicket snapped closed.

"Oh! Oh!" screamed the girl. She came running, clutching for Jigger's arm, and looking behind her.

As she reached his side she swung about and fired blindly.

The thunderous report of the heavy-calibered pistol was deafening. The recoil jarred the little weapon out of her hand. It fell to the floor—and immediately exploded a second time. The slug ricocheted and whined from wall to wall, but did no harm.

Turning, Jigger did not quite have time to shift his own weapon and fire, as Miss Ingalls got in the way. But the glimpse he got was sufficient to freeze the blood in his arteries.

On the inside wall of the gallery a wide panel had opened. In dimensions it was perhaps six feet by two, as nearly as he could judge in that wild, jostling, desperate moment.

Framed in that panel were six hideous faces. They were Oriental faces—yet not human! Great smooth bulges across the line of cheekbones left the slant eyes above deep-sunken, and the mouths were gashes of thin-lipped scarlet.

Not one of the leering, sinister faces had a nose!

10

THE RAT

EVERY LIGHT IN the room went out.

Jigger Masters, holding the trembling girl with his left arm, swept her sidewise.

Sudden, overpowering rage against this society or dreaded tong swayed his better judgment. Still facing toward that panel in the wall, he leveled the automatic and blazed away thrice in rapid succession. Then he ducked low to the floor, still holding Miss Ingalls, and changed position several feet.

"No go," he said harshly. "They aren't there now—panel closed!"

"What is this horrible thing? What are we—doing?" It was evident that she still moved in a daze of unreality; that only one fact came to her as a solace. This man, this stranger, was trying to help her against that gang of noseless things with the scaly claws....

"Don't leave me," she whispered, terrified. He had not answered—for what was there to answer? Out of the dark something would come. And he was under no illusions now. He himself had been warned not to interfere. When he had gone ahead, as of course they must have known he would do, he had been sentenced.

The terrible doom promised was not this yellow fungus—though the stuffing of his body with the loathsome streamers of parasite might follow the regular entertainment provided, he supposed. From his reading he had found this sign of the setting sun a little bit familiar, when he had first seen it on one of the slips of laundry paper. It had haunted his mind, barely escaping him.

It had needed only the addition of the silhouetted rat to bring back clearly a memory of what it might portend to him.

"I won't leave you—willingly," he said; but the last word was inaudible to her. "I'd like to make sure that one of these two doors is open… I'll crawl over there on my hands and knees."

"I'll crawl, too. Can't we get through to the stairs now? You must have come in that way."

"Do you know how to make them swing down?" he asked eagerly. Keeping his whisper so nearly noiseless that he had to bend very close to make her hear. Little by little they were progressing across the rug, past the table, in the direction, supposedly, of one of the doors, now invisible.

"No. Granddad always kept that his own secret. Nothing out in the rooms to control them, as far as I know. I was always—scared they might fold up and leave me here. Scared!" She gave a ghost of a laugh. "I never knew what fright really was!"

"Were you the one who waved? Where is that small window I saw?"

"I was desperate. They were up here. Every time I tried to get out and downstairs, one of those awful people without noses—" She held his arm convulsively. "How can we ever get away? Three of those little windows are in each of these rooms, but they won't open now."

"Why not?"

"They are electrically controlled. Everything in this house moves by means of small motors set in the walls. There are oiled chains and sprocket gears. I've seen a few of them when they were out of order. Murphy and Granddad did most of the repairing. Sometimes Claude Gerlach, the chauffeur, helped. But now all the lights are out. That means the current has been turned off at the master switches. Nothing will open—or if it's already open, nothing will close!"

At that second they reached the wall, and Masters felt the sill of the door. He reached upward, tried the knob. It did not yield. He tried one after another of the brass keys he had pocketed. In vain.

"None works," he whispered. "I'm afraid that we're in for it. Do you suppose you could find one of those wall windows? I might succeed in prying one open, even if the electrical catch did not work."

"But no one can get out of there. They are too small." Her voice, husky and with a renewed tremor, sounded as though she were on the verge of hysteria.

He got the girl to her feet, and together on tiptoe they groped a way to the curved outside wall.

"I have a small flash, but I'd rather not use it except in an emergency," he said. "See if you can locate one of those windows. I have some tools, though I think they're too delicate for any sort of forcing. If there's any sort of a lock, though—"

MINUTES PASSED, WITH no interruption. The detective had been keyed up to high pitch. Yet when nothing happened he relaxed slightly and began to hope. Possibly Gildersleeve had managed to break into the Brick Wart, and was even now downstairs. When he listened it seemed he could discern vague noises from below stairs. Yet he dared not shout, for fear matters would be precipitated. Given only time enough, it was certain that Tom Gildersleeve would take the brick fortress apart wall by wall, if he believed Jigger Masters a prisoner there.

And he could believe nothing else now. It would be far better, however, if some line of communication could be established. This window, now—

Minutes of examination proved the hopelessness of trying to open this. The button control was dead. On the inside, a whole plug of wall a foot in depth, much like the plug which is taken out of a watermelon when testing for ripeness, was supposed to jump out when the catch was clicked open. By reaching in an arm then, a lever latch could be thrown, and the window opened outwards. At this time, however, with electricity all over the house stopped, the hidden lock did not give when the button was pressed. There was practically no crack, none large enough, at any rate, to furnish leverage. A man would need a pick or drill, in order to force it.

Outside of these three port hole windows, there was just one opening. This was the ventilator of the air-conditioning system, set low on the inside wall at one corner, and covered with a camouflage grating. Masters determined that no air was coming in at this aperture at present, doubtless owing to the cessation of electric current. He wondered grimly how long it would take to exhaust the oxygen in this small gallery, but said nothing of it to Lois Ingalls.

"Come over this way," he whispered, guiding her to the central curve of the outside wall. "We'll just have to sit down here and wait—watching that panel across. In order to attack us they'll have to turn on the lights. Then—well, I have five shots left. Our big hope lies in help from outside. But now, Miss Ingalls—"

"Oh, call me Lois," she said. "I—I'd hate to die so formally!" Was there the veriest hint of a laugh in her words? The poise and courage of this girl were splendid.

Here at this moment, faced with the grimmest likelihood that he would never be permitted to leave the Brick Wart, even to look once at Lois Ingalls in the sunlight, he felt the strongest possible urge to take her in his arms.

Jigger did put his left arm over the girl's right shoulder, clasping her left forearm and drawing her close.

She whispered, "I feel so much—safer!"

"Suppose you tell me all about this queer affair, everything you know about the house here, Seth Bryson, and what kind of monkey business he has got himself involved in. I suppose he *is* somewhere around here in this house—"

"I think so," she breathed. "When you came in, didn't you see him? How did you get in, if you didn't?"

Masters told her tersely of his intimidation of Murphy. "But I have a background of other happenings," he said then. "The trail of murder and vandalism led to this house. Now I have reason to think that Mr. Bryson is either a member of this band that goes around smashing up Ming porcelain, or else is another one of its intended victims.

Tell me, has your grandfather any considerable collection of Chinese porcelains—or indeed, any of them at all?"

"Yes, indeed. This very room—I can't imagine what's become of them! There were more than a score of pieces here, and some of them worth thousands of dollars. When I came in here, dusting—you know, Granddad would not let anyone but me do it—I saw that every one of those pieces was gone. Stolen. That was when those—those monsters came!" She shivered and drew closer to his shoulder.

"Let's go back. I want to know about you—and your grandfather. How long have you been with him?"

"Six years—since my mother died." She stopped. There had been a faint, sighing sound which appeared to come from the room itself. Masters also heard it. The pistol was ready, however. He could make no greater preparation.

In the darkness he could not know that the small wicket aperture through which the deadly bamboo tube had come at an earlier moment, had opened again. What poked into the blackness of the chamber now was not the same bamboo tube, but a hoselike contrivance. From it came first a sighing, then an almost inaudible rushing sound....

She made a queer sound, halfway between a yawn and a moan. "I feel so sleepy—sleepy. Do you think I might lay my head on your shoulder—and—and—"

"No!" cried Masters suddenly. He got to his feet in a hurry. All of a sudden the significance of that faint rushing sound had come to him, and he nearly shouted his horror at the certainty that this pleasant numbing sensation stealing over his own body was to be accounted for in just one way—*gas.*

"They're coming!" he cried. As he stood erect, lifting Lois

Ingalls to her feet and feeling how she slumped dazedly against him, he got a fuller breath of the almost odorless gas. He choked a little. And then the lights flashed on!

The panel where the noseless Chinamen had been was closed. There was no one in the room... no one....

He caught himself as he reeled, trying to hold his breath. Somewhere there was gas... coming... and they must... stop... it....

Then goggling, as the veins in his forehead seemed to swell and make it difficult to see anything clearly, he managed to make out the fact that some kind of hose nozzle projected into the room from that open wicket.

Too late. By a prodigious effort, letting go his hold on the girl so she promptly slumped in a heap on the rug, he staggered around, trying to lift his pistol to shoot out the gas nozzle as he had shot away the bamboo tube.

He could not lift the heavy weapon, which seemed all of a sudden to weigh a ton. Staggering, his head falling forward, he gripped his right wrist with his left hand, forcing up... up... the muzzle toward its target.

Whammm!

He had pulled the trigger. But that once would be all. He tried to see whether or not he had been successful, but unable to pierce the mists that came over his vision. His knees sagged. The automatic fell from his loosening fingers.

With a final groaning gasp of an iron will that fought to the last ditch, he fell to hands and knees, then face forward to the rug beside the girl he had come to save.

ON THE INNER wall of the gallery, where Masters had glimpsed the noseless men in what appeared to be a six-foot panel, the seemingly solid wall opened. It was the "panel"—but now it revealed itself as a doorway. The door, which was all a part of the finished wall, split horizontally here for a width of six feet. Sliding smoothly down, to end with a clank, the door disappeared into a slot in the floor.

Through this wide aperture stepped four Chinese. They were in American clothes—all wearing blue serge. They were hatless, and had their black hair cut American style. On their hands were yellow gloves finished with scales and claws to look like talons of a fabled dragon.

And over their faces from neck to cheekbones were tight-fitting masks—gas masks. The parted lips on these masks were nothing more than red paint—and a fine filter screen for what seemed at a distance to be teeth.

Not a sound was made by their felt slippers. No words were spoken, naturally. A brief sign from the first of the quartet caused the metal hose to close with a hissing squawk, and be withdrawn. The wicket closed.

Two of the Orientals bent and lifted the limp body of Lois Ingalls, and carried her out through the open door. The others waited impassively, looking down at the uncon-scious body of Jigger Masters. There came a faint singing noise, made by an electric elevator. This stopped, began again, stopped. The two remaining Chinese stooped and took Masters by wrists and ankles. They did not bother to lift him, but dragged him across the polished floor, out of the gallery, and into a small automatic elevator.

The sliding door rose from its floor slot, and clanked closed. The elevator descended slowly, making its singing sound.

"HE IS AWAKENING now. In a moment we shall apply restorative measures which will bring his brain and sensitivity back to normal. First, however, Miss Ingalls, I wish to point out to you how dreadful a thing it is for you to refuse to save the life of a good man, an American man of not much more than your own age."

The suave, persuasive voice was that of a small, wizened Chinaman. He alone of all the tong members was unmasked, and wore the sweeping white mustache, the queue, the brocaded mandarin jacket and the roomy trousers of his native dress.

Among his countrymen this cultured, quiet-seeming man had a name of royalty. But out in Chicago where he had occasional dealings with white men—some of them vice lords, some of them earnest, grim-faced men whose lives were chanced in the fight against dope, kidnaping and racketeering—he used another name.

It was a curious name, Wun Wey. Perhaps it was Oriental humor, a rendering into phonetic English a hint of the business in which the Illustrious Society of Executioners had been engaged for centuries. At any rate it was a name which could bring sudden terror to any Chinaman in America.

"It lies in your power, Miss Ingalls, to save this man," repeated Wun Wey. He stood with arms folded, the long-nailed hands concealed in the black silk sleeves of his ornate jacket.

Before him were two zinc-topped tables, evidently part of the normal furnishings of this long laboratory or workshop.

On one of the zinc tables lay Jigger Masters, moving uneasily now under his restraining bonds. As Wun Wey suggested, he was nearing consciousness after his dose of anaesthetic gas. His tongue came out part of an inch and tried to wet his dry lips.

To his left lay Lois Ingalls, bound as she had been bound up in the attic room where Masters had found her. She was not gagged now; but the staring terror and the pallor of her cheeks testified to speechlessness and an agony of fear.

Why, oh, why could these yellow men not let her and Masters free? As she had assured Wun Wey a dozen times, she would have told him anything in the world he wanted to know—only she did not have the faintest conception of his meaning. Manuals? Watered silk manuals? What in the world were they?

"I know nothing of what you mean! Nothing!" she cried, hysteria mingling with passion. "Why can't you get that through your head? My grandfather never told me a word about anything like a manual. I don't know what it *is!*"

The last word came shrill. She could see from the old Celestial's impassivity that he did not believe. Or perhaps he really did believe. In which case he would go ahead with the horrible things he promised, just on the remote shred of a chance that after all his judgment might be proved wrong in extremity.

"This man Masters," continued Wun Wey imperturbably, "could be counted our deadly enemy. The honored society to which I belong, however, never takes any one mere mortal so seriously. We know this man is a good member of your western society. And so now, provided we attain our object in coming here, we are disposed to be merciful. If you will tell us where those manuals have been hidden, we will let this man go free—and you will not have his death upon your mind and soul all the rest of your life. Otherwise—"

"Don't believe a word he says, Lois," breathed Jigger Masters. "As long as you don't tell him, you may live—though I think both of us are doomed. You gave us the saffron death, didn't you?" he asked Wun Wey grimly.

The Chinaman shook his head. "No, we did not," he replied. "That would have been done, but misfortune intervened. And now our plans are slightly changed. That was a harmless anaesthetic gas which you and Miss Ingalls inhaled. Beyond a slight headache, perhaps, you will suffer no ill effects. The gas is cocanal, in case you wish to know. But I have no time to waste. You will urge your companion, Mr. Masters, to tell us what we need to know, or else—"

"Why don't you go to Seth Bryson?" demanded the detective. "You have him here somewhere, and I should think this matter concerned him and you, not Miss Ingalls."

The slant eyes narrowed with cold cruelty. "We have Mr. Bryson," said the Chinaman, without emphasis. "Unfortunately there has been a little mismanagement of his—ah—entertainment. He cannot speak."

"OH-H, YOU'VE KILLED him!" gasped Lois.

"No," said Wun Wey. "He is merely unconscious, and measures are being taken to revive him. They may not be successful. We would not grieve if they failed, if only Miss Ingalls would tell—"

"But I don't know!" she cried despairingly. "I haven't the faintest idea—"

"Enough! We shall see if a realization of what you are causing Mr. Masters to endure will not help your failing memory. You see," sneered Wun Wey, "we have positive knowledge that you have been in the confidence of Mr. Bryson for several years. Very well, you will talk now—or consider yourself forever as a murderess!"

Wun Wey turned from them. Withdrawing one skinny hand on which the five-inch fingernails were encased in silver sheaths, he gestured briefly. As though they had been awaiting that signal, two masked Chinese entered the room, noiseless on their felt slippers.

One of the two bore a small silver bowl, perhaps nine inches in diameter and three inches deep. The bottom of this bowl was recessed for a half-inch—a matter of sinister importance, as was soon to develop. This Chinaman also carried a stoppered silver flask.

The second masked Oriental bore a curious object, one which caused the lips of Jigger Masters to straighten them-selves into a harsh, set line. The object was a trap cage of wire. In the cage was a single full grown rat. He knew now that his guess at the significance of the setting sun and silhouetted rat had been correct.

"Oh—what is *that?*" cried Lois in a husky, terrified voice. "I give you my solemn word, Mr. Masters, I don't know what he asks! Can't you make him believe it?"

"It would make no difference, I think," said Jigger Masters. "It is not your fight—Lois. And if—if this is the end of things, I'd like to have known you—better."

Like trained automatons the two Chinese stepped forward. The one with the bowl tore Master's shirt exposing his chest and his flat, muscled abdomen. On this was placed the silver bowl, inverted. The Chinaman unstoppered the flask, and poured two or three ounces of a pungent, colorless liquid into the recessed bottom of the inverted bowl, and struck a match. The liquid flamed upward with a greenish-yellow fire!

Wun Wey himself now took the rat cage. "You see, Miss Ingalls," he said dryly, "I slip the rat under the fiery bowl—thus!" And he opened the back of the cage, with a dexterous motion trapping the rodent underneath the flaming bowl. "In a moment or two the creature will begin to feel the uncomfortable heat. Then he will try harder to escape his small and stifling prison. He has long, sharp teeth, of course. And the only way he can hope to chew a way to freedom, will be downward...."

Even Masters himself grimaced then. Was that peculiar rubbing sensation the first bite of the hot rat?

With a single gasping cry of utter horror, Lois Ingalls fainted.

Masters saw, and his frame tautened. From somewhere downstairs came the voices of men he knew!

Shouted calls for him. And they came deafeningly, quite as though Gildersleeve and the other man were right in the next room.

Then Masters understood. This was a microphone and announcer. Well, perhaps it worked both ways, though he doubted it. Glancing over just once to make sure that Lois Ingalls still lay unconscious he allowed his features to contort as if in terrible agony. Then bellow after bellow burst from his chest and throat.

One of the masked Chinese moved uneasily, but Wun Wey shook his head to the silent question. "No one can hear his agony," he said. "It is of no use, or we could revive the girl. I believe now that she does not know. This man, however, has merited death. He is clever in his own way, and an obstacle to be removed. Strange… I do not recognize genuine pain in your cries, Mr. Masters." Wun Wey looked puzzled. He took a step or two forward, withdrew a yellow hand from his sleeve, and touched the back of it to the silver bowl.

"Ah, yes, the bowl is hot."

Masters was emitting explosive yowls. If any sounds at all could reach the ears of Tom Gildersleeve, these must. But he feared only too greatly that Wun Wey spoke the truth.

At length Masters detected a flicker of the long eyelashes and a movement of the face muscles on Lois Ingalls' countenance. Promptly he throttled down the hideous yells, into gasps, then almost soundless groans, then silence. He feigned unconsciousness himself, though he knew Wun Wey, frowning down now, was not deceived.

He turned, jabbering out a shrill sentence in Chinese.

One of the masked men with scaly gloves glided forward, reaching for the silver bowl on which the volatile fluid had just about burned out. He whisked away the bowl.

There on Jigger's abdomen lay the body of a dead rat.

11

HEEL OF ACHILLES

FOR THE SPACE of several heartbeats Wun Wey was shocked and surprised into silence. Jigger grinned up at him, then turned and deliberately winked at Lois, who watched, her blue eyes horrified. The wink brought an expression of bewilderment and relief to her face. Masters wanted her to imagine this was no more than a hoax, when he himself realized full well that he had gained through forethought and accurate guessing no more than a few minutes reprieve.

Wun Wey turned his slitted eyes full upon Masters. The Chinaman's face itself was inscrutable, but a fire either of intense anger or awakened admiration burned in the black eyes. Wun Wey turned his head and jabbered shrill commands to one of his helpers.

That one advanced, scraped with one scaly claw at the skin over Jigger's stomach, and then exclaimed with squeaky satisfaction. By bending his neck Jigger saw the masked man pull up the edge of the sheet of collodion, and then tear it away little by little, much as a mustard plaster is torn off. The process was slightly painful.

Wun Wey sniffed briefly once at the sheet of solidified

collodion, and then he knew. Prussic acid has an odor that persists.

"Ah, the odor of bitter almonds," he breathed softly. "The rat gnawed—but did not live long enough after that, to break the skin! You are a more brilliant enemy than even I deemed, Mr. Masters. I wonder—"

He paused, seemingly lost in reflection.

"Let the girl go," Jigger burst out. "Then do whatever you've got in your dirty mind, as far as I'm concerned. I discounted dying, a long while ago when I started to hunt down vermin like yourself!"

"I'll stay with you," cried the girl.

"Thank you," said Jigger. "But I'm afraid we're not free agents. This ex-laundryman—" Jigger, made the terms just as offensive as he could— "this Shensi coolie intends to kill me. He is incapable of understanding the truth, so all we can hope is that his childish brain will see no gain in holding you. That would be—"

Wun Wey did not respond as Jigger hoped.

"That is all nonsense, Mr. Masters, as you know," he said mildly. "Let Miss Ingalls go free? Ah, we will have to think about that."

"I don't see any possible benefit to you in holding her," lied Masters bravely. In his own mind there came up sharply a vision of using Lois as a method of persuading old Bryson to surrender this secret he appeared to have clasped tightly to his bosom. But Jigger hoped that this weapon had not occurred to the Chinaman.

He might have spared himself the bother.

"Oh, there could be many benefits, even to one as old and shrunken as myself," returned the Oriental placidly.

"But the immediate object of my society is one we must not forget. Sooner or later those stupid men upstairs will break a way into this basement, if they do not find the stairs or elevator. I propose to make you my ambassador, Mr. Masters!"

"Eh?" Jigger looked astonished.

"I know you will comprehend my explanation," said Wun Wey placidly, "so I shall speak very briefly. Ten years ago Seth Bryson travelled in China. While there he bribed a minor priest in one of the lamaseries, a member then of my order, to steal two articles for him. These are manuals, directions for a certain process told in ideographs on watered silk. Each manual is rolled. It is four inches long, and one inch thick on its spindle.

"I shall not explain what process is embodied on the manuals. It would be best, in case you accept my offer, not to be curious. My society is pledged to erase from the earth all men—and women—who have learned this. I have come to think that Miss Ingalls actually does not know; and for that reason only I make the sincere offer to spare her life—on conditions.

"Right now we shall take her away with us, to the safe place where we have her grandfather. You will be left with a free hand, for a certain time. As free a hand with this Bryson house as the police will allow, at any rate. *You will search and find those manuals for us!*"

The Chinaman's voice ended.

"**HOW DO YOU** expect me to succeed when you have failed?" Jigger asked calmly, though his brain raced.

"You will *have* to! This is your chosen field, discovering hidden things. Very well. I will reverse what I said earlier to Miss Ingalls. You will use your knowledge of men—Americans, and especially criminals like Seth Bryson—to imagine *where* in this house he hid those manuals! If you do not find them, Miss Ingalls will suffer the Death of a Thousand Slices!"

"Good God!" The words burst like a groan from Masters, and he felt cold perspiration start at his temples. "Look here, Chinaman, wouldn't my solemn word be enough? Wouldn't you let Miss Ingalls go, if I promised on my word of honor to find those damned things—if it were at all humanly possible?"

"We are not interested in mercy," countered Wun Wey coldly. "In fact our business is death. But we are ready to bargain—and we always keep our bargains. We doubt that you will find those two manuals, since we have failed. The grasping devil who stole them utilized Satanic ingenuity in hiding them.

You will drive your brain and your body through hell-fire, however, to save the white, satiny breast of Miss Ingalls from the caress of those delicate, beautiful knives with the sharp lips...."

"Oh, don't! I can't *stand* it!" cried the girl hysterically. "Find them, won't you, Mr. Masters? Oh, I—I'm so afraid!"

"I'll find them," he promised. "No matter where Bryson hid them, I'll find them. Let me up."

"Speedily," nodded the Chinaman, well satisfied.

He issued sharp, crackling commands. Two masked men came, loosed the girl's bonds, and carried her away.

Another subordinate came with a portable cylinder with a hose and nozzle attached. Wun Wey held him back an instant.

"We trust no one," said the Celestial coldly. "You will awaken in ten minutes, and find yourself free to search. See to it that you succeed before high noon of the second day from now. We are leaving, how you will not know. Miss Ingalls will go with us. Over there on the east wall"—he pointed—"is the button for the elevator and those for the two folding stairs. The other passageways and locks are controlled by a switchboard in the middle stairway well.

"When you want to exchange the manuals with us for Miss Ingalls, walk around the block here wearing a yellow tie. Before high noon, of the second day. You will be accosted."

ELEVEN MINUTES LATER, to the gasped astonishment of the Hempstead police and Tom Gildersleeve, Jigger Masters, pale and strained of countenance, stepped out of the panel opening which hid the electric elevator at the first floor landing.

"The house is ours now," he said hoarsely. "They have gone—escaped. And I have until noon of the second day...."

12

SPUTTERING DEATH

"TELL ME, GIL, just what's happened here,"Masters said. "Then I've got something to tell you."

The chunky assistant was impatient. He wanted Masters to lead them instantly against this mysterious foe, and thought little or nothing of his side of the story. Yet it contained matters of absorbing interest to Jigger Masters.

The police had come, reinforced by Connor from Mineola. They had found the bronze door closed; and no one answered the bell. From across the street, however, one watcher posted to keep an eye on the roof saw one of the small upstairs windows open, and a weird figure framed for just a few seconds in the aperture.

"I tell you," said Gildersleeve huskily, "it looked like a man or a monkey that didn't have a nose! And I knew *you* were inside the Wart, mebbe fighting that very thing! We didn't bother with ceremonies then. We come in—with pickaxes!

"Inside the place we come on this butler fella, Murphy. He was all choking up, same as Marriott and Tomeroy. Doc Cortelyou rushed him over to the hospital at Mineola. Says if blood tests show the bugs he'll give Murphy that new-fangled radio fever treatment to try and kill 'em. Says it's a wild chance, but the only one he knows."

"Thank God there's that much!" said Jigger grimly. "There more than likely will be others of us who will need it. But go on. Hurry. What else?" He seemed to hold himself back in the chair by sheer will power. The faintness had gone.

Only one more item of importance emerged from the narrative. The police, searching through the adjacent grounds as well as those of the Brick Wart, found a Packard limousine in the garage of the house next door. The house was empty. No chauffeur was in evidence.

"But that's the car old Yancey saw Jones take," said Gil earnestly. "Jones was that fella on crutches who bought the jugs an' fancy art ware at the galleries, you remember. An' the number on the plates is the same one that's registered for Seth Bryson!"

"His car, of course," nodded Jigger. "Wish you could find that chauffeur. Call in this Sergeant Milbank and the rest. I've got to tell them the strangest and most terrible yarn they ever heard!"

In a minute all the others, including Milbank and Lieutenant Connor, crowded back into the room where they had left Masters with Gildersleeve. Striding back and forth in his own grim stress of worry and excitement, he sketched briefly for them the happenings inside the Brick Wart since the moment of his own arrival.

"What I know now does not fully explain the deaths of Kagodi, Marriott and Tomeroy," he admitted. "It's linked up with the Ming porcelains and the manuals that fiend Wun Wey demands, somehow.

*Compressing the bellows, he drove out
a thick gray cloud of the dust.*

"Certain it is that Seth Bryson, who has lived in this fortress of a house, hiding from the Chinese whom he despoiled ten years ago, deserves little sympathy. But he is probably dying right now. We are forced to ignore his plight—until Miss Lois Ingalls is safe.

"Everything fades before that one thing. I must save her from the Death of the Thousand Slices! Once that is done, we will stamp out the hideous Tao Tong forever. We must find these manuals. They are probably small rolls of silk—maybe four inches long—covered with Chinese ideographs. Somewhere in this house they are hidden...."

A FERMENTATION OF activity churned inside Bryson's bizarre house, Brick Wart.

Sergeant Milbank and his men took charge of the

minute search of the first floor. Lieutenant Connor and
Detective Sergeant Emerson from Mineola strode up to
the attic floor. They would empty every vase, urn and other
receptacle, hunt for possible wall caches, safes or other
hiding places.

Jigger Masters, pale and determined, took Tom Gildersleeve with him to the immense, high-ceilinged basement.

"Hello—this is a second laboratory." Masters had
opened a green enamelled door similar to the one at the
head of the gallery stair well, and now looked into a long
room identical in shape with the other laboratory in which
he had been held prisoner for a time.

This room, however, was devoted to drying racks for
pottery, a plumber's testing apparatus.

In it was one exhibit, however, which caused exclama-
tions to burst from the throats of both men. In a corner on
a zinc table, and spilled off to the floor on both sides, was
a heap of pulverized white stuff which both Gil and Jigger
Masters recognized at a glance. Here was where the valuable porcelain that had been in that third-floor gallery of
Bryson's had disappeared! The Chinese most evidently had
carried it down, then carefully pounded it to dust.

"I can understand just about everything except this!"
said Masters in a hushed voice. "Why would they want
to destroy many thousands of dollars' worth of antique
pottery?"

"Beyond me," said Gil. "Say, what's that funny wall?"

The wall to which he directed attention was irregularly
built, in no place more than four feet in height, and apparently constructed of pieces of colored tile no two of which
were alike in hue or texture.

"This man Bryson was no slouch in his own line," said Masters, half to himself. "He seems to have tried his hand at making about everything, from porous brick to this beautiful tile. See the big blue piece?" he added, touching an equilateral triangle which was as smooth and glossy to the touch as the most expensive plate glass. "It's either genuine Multan from India or so good an imitation that I'd never know the difference."

He suddenly stopped, stiffening, and a peculiar light came into the hazel eyes. "I wonder!" he breathed. The detective went on, frowning, looking more swiftly through this laboratory room, then continuing with the rest of the basement where the air conditioner, the oil furnace, and the laundries were located. Beyond the latter they found a thermostatically-controlled cool room, where on built-in wall shelves hundreds of bottles of vintage wines lay on their sides.

"Get Sergeant Millbank and three-four patrolmen," Masters ordered. "The walls, ceiling and floor all have to be tested for hollow sounds. They might as well get started on these rooms we've surveyed. I'm expecting to have to spend a lot more time in the other laboratory, the one from which the Chinese disappeared."

"You think there's another way out?" queried Gil.

"Has to be! Oh, and say," Masters glanced at his wrist watch and grimaced at the swift flight of the hours. "Two thirty. Have them make some black coffee upstairs, and bring down a pot and cup for me."

"All right, chief. Any chow?"

"Anything," said Masters, "as long as I can carry it along

with me, and eat as I look. I'm going into the other lab now."

Gildersleeve hurried away to the elevator, to return fifteen minutes later with a pot of coffee and a heaping tray of sandwiches. "They sure eat well in the Bryson household," he said. "I did this myself, and I had the choice of pretty nearly everything that hungry man ever used in a sandwich. Have fun! Milbank is going over the wine closet."

Cup and sandwich in his hands, the detective ate hungrily as he passed slowly about one end of the second laboratory. Aware of the fact that the Chinese had been in possession of the Wart for at least one day, he had no hopes of finding Seth Bryson's cache the first time over the ground. The Orientals must have exhausted all their imagination.

Three cups of the coffee had disappeared, and Gildersleeve was piling the plates and saucers on the empty tray when there came a sharp cry from Masters. He was bending over one of the long and deep vats which appeared to have had for their purpose the laving of pottery—perhaps the washing with the engobe coat which is put on many sorts of ceramic ware before glazing, much as a coat of size is put on wood or other wall surfaces before applying paint or enamel.

Silently putting down the tray, Gil came immediately.

"What *is* it? You've found somep'n'?" he demanded.

"I think so," said Masters, frowning. He took out a jack-knife and a used envelope from his pocket. Bending over the side of the vat he used the blade of the knife to scrape off something brownish yellow—something that looked like a high-water mark in the vat. But as Gildersleeve leaned closer also to see, he gasped and his gray-blue eyes fairly boggled.

"*The saffron death!*" he cried. "That's the fungus. Look out, and don't get your fingers on it!"

In stern and puzzled silence Jigger Masters looked down at the soggy bit of spongy yellow stuff, balanced on the envelope.

"It certainly looks like it. You'll have to take it to Dr. Cortelyou and have him put it under the mike, though," he said slowly. "Now what in the name of all the serene sacred sea lions?

"Hm, the pieces of our puzzle don't fit... not yet, anyhow. This vat has been used for the yellow fungus. Perhaps it has been cultured here. But if so, that means either that the Chinese have been in possession of this house much longer than any of us has reason to believe, or else that Seth Bryson himself has a hand in using this stuff—"

"With that gang double-crossing him at the end?" queried Gildersleeve doubtfully. "Well, you've seen this girl, Miss Ingalls. D'you suppose she could have lived here six years and not know about the Chinese? Or that she... she herself...."

"Never that!" Jigger said with emphasis. "I suppose that the zoöspores of the fungus would culture swiftly in a vat. This stuff might have been mixed here recently, though that yellow rim looks like it has been on this tub for quite a while... Gil, I have an idea! But it can wait. We've got to find the manuals first."

HOURS PASSED, WITH the search for the mysterious and hidden manuals proceeding. Another *al fresco* meal, cooked and served by the police, was eaten. Outside morning was beginning to break. A continuous din of thumping, pounding, punctuated by crashes of falling shelves of books, tinware in the kitchens, even to pieces of crockery or art objects resounded within the Brick Wart.

And with the exception of the outside secret passages under the eaves and between Seth Bryson's suite and all the other downstairs rooms, no new discoveries had been made. Through with the third floor, Lieutenant Connor was now working on Lois Ingalls' suite and the other rooms of the second floor.

Dr. Cortelyou had come back from the hospital, bearing the news of Murphy the butler's death from the fungus. Setting up the radio fever apparatus had taken too long a time. In spite of that, however, the medical examiner was far from downcast.

"I halted the damned growth," he said hoarsely to Masters. "Now the oscillator is all set up and will stay that way. I can raise the bodily temperature of any patient to 106 degrees and keep it there just as long as I want. That murders the saprophytes, blows 'em up. I think I can check this horrible stuff."

"So if any more of us get inoculated?" demanded Jigger sharply. His face was lined with hours of concentration, but this was apt to be all too pressing a problem at any moment they managed to catch up with the dread Tao Tong. What he really feared was that even if he found the manuals, and exchanged them for the safety of Lois Ingalls, those saturnine devils would deliver her to him apparently all right. Safe and sound—but with the horrible zoöspores in her blood, a lurking death which would claim her in a few hours in spite of everything they could do.

"I'm all ready to work," snapped Cortelyou, "but I make no absolute promises. You expect to have more patients?"

"I hope and pray not—but I'm afraid of it," said Masters grimly. "I want you where you can be reached instantly."

"I live only a half-mile from the hospital at Mineola. Phone me when you start there with a patient, and I'll be waiting for you."

So the doctor yawned, shook hands with Masters, and took his departure.

Again in the second laboratory with Gildersleeve, Jigger Masters wrestled with ideas which came more and more slowly. At first he had thought out possible hiding places in relation to the rooms and the apparatus faster even than he could test them. Now, however, he was nearing the conclusion that Seth Bryson could not have hidden those precious manuals in the basement.

A horrible thought had come to make him clench his fists. As he understood the situation, from that short and one-sided talk with the Chinese headman, these two watered silk manuals described a secret process which had something to do with ceramics. Seth Bryson, traveling in China—and doubtless buying or stealing antique pottery as he went—had hired a minor priest or lama to get him these precious manuals. After having the manuals in his possession long enough so he could test out and memorize the process involved, would it not be the natural thing for Bryson to destroy them?

Then this desperate search and attempt to save Lois Ingalls from a hideous death was futile.

"I won't believe it!" said Jigger doggedly, glaring at the laboratory walls. Gildersleeve watched him with red, fatigued eyes. "We'll have to get another string to our bow, Gil. Those manuals may have been destroyed. At any rate it doesn't look like we're going to find them. Then we'll have to find the Chinese. Where have they gone?"

"They must have gone through a tunnel leading out," said Gildersleeve.

"Of course!" snapped Masters. "Bryson used every secret lock, alarm, secret passage, folding stair, and other device he could have built in, so he would be protected against this very tong. Probably had a back way to escape in case the Chinese managed to win a way inside his defenses. But where is the escape, and where are the Chinese now?"

Gildersleeve scowled.

"A crowd of Chinese with their two captives must take up some tangible space," Masters went on. "Also that automobile of Bryson's. You say it's kept next door. At the house on which side?"

"That way!" said Gil, pointing west.

Masters, looking thoughtful, followed by Gildersleeve, went directly up to the room where four Hempstead patrolmen were lounging, two of them sound asleep, the others able to open an eye apiece and look at this tireless detective machine who now came with new demands and questions concerning the neighbors who lived next door to the Brick Wart.

That way? In the little white house? Oh, that was only a cripple—a fella who'd got jimmed up in an airplane crash some three-four years back. Name of Michael Maher—yeah, Irish. Used a crutch when he walked at all. Lived alone with one manservant who was named Claude Gerlach—

"Claude Gerlach!" echoed Masters from between taut lips. This was the name, according to Lois Ingalls, of *their* chauffeur.

"And what color hair has Mr. Maher?" demanded Jigger, certain that he knew the forthcoming answer. It was under this identity that Seth Bryson had gone forth on his pottery-buying trips to the Yancey Galleries.

"What color wud any good Irishman be havin'?" demanded Officer Casey with a grin, putting on more brogue than he used ordinarily. "Carrot red, bedad! An'why are ye interested in ould Mike Maher? Though he ain't so ould, mebbe, I dunno."

But Masters had wheeled. Seizing Gildersleeve and Connor, who had just come in, by the arms, he took them with him. The elevator to the basement was so small they were flattened like sardines in a can.

In the basement Masters pointed toward the end of the first laboratory. "The white house where the Packard is kept is in that direction," he said tersely. "There must be a door and a tunnel passage somewhere. Find them!"

But it was Masters himself who finally gave a stifled cry, and then turned, face white.

"It's here—a crack!" he whispered. "There's a bit of movable tile, too, but I can't make the thing open of itself. I'm going to pry. Have your guns ready. No telling, if we open this, what we'll find beyond. I don't believe, though, that I want an open fight unless there's no other way...."

With a hand crowbar then he worked as noiselessly as possible. The bit of movable tile fell out, leaving a space two inches wide, ideal for leverage. With a gentle pressure a tall, narrow door outlined itself, though the jointure had been done so perfectly that no sign of it had been apparent heretofore, except at the tiny spot where the tile moved.

"There's some kind of a catch on the other side," whispered the detective. "Be ready. I'm going to force it!"

There came a rubbing *snap*. The door came silently open, revealing a narrow six-foot tunnel ending in blackness ahead.

And one more thing was shown—something terrifying! Just in front of Jigger's face, but sputtering downwards towards the floor at the swift rate of one foot a second, was a length of ignited "instantaneous" fuse.

His action then was almost automatic, and takes more time in telling than in performance.

With a sudden leap forward he seized the unburned portion of fuse, yanking at it to tear it away from the explosive he knew instantly must be hidden somewhere below them.

In vain. The fuse was strong. He saw that it went down to a hole drilled in the floor of the tunnel. Then the flaming sputter reached his hand, searing.

Dropping to his knees, grabbing out his jackknife, he managed to get to sawing there just four inches above the floor.

No time! The terrific speed of the fuse was uncanny. The fire was only eighteen inches away... ten inches....

"Run for your lives!" Jigger cried to Connor and Tom Gildersleeve.

Then he bent his head to the spot he had cut, chewing, soaking the tough fuse with saliva. It was the last chance.

There came a stinging burn on the side of his mouth, on his tongue....

13

THE GOAD OF DESPERATION

FOR A FULL, slow second, as he continued to chew on
the hot fuse, Jigger Masters did not know whether he had
quenched the fire or not. His mouth pained. At last he
jerked the still unbroken fuse from his mouth and sawed
through it with his jackknife.

"Thank God for that!" breathed Lieutenant Connor. He
and Tom Gildersleeve stood there, beaded with perspiration on their foreheads. They both held revolvers, and now
peered ahead into the blackness of the tunnel. But neither
one of them was half as frightened of the yellow murderers who must be ahead in the other house somewhere as
he had been of that sputtering menace.

"You're a pair of damned fools," said Jigger softly. "Why
didn't you run when you had the chance?"

"I couldn't've run," admitted Gil dryly. "My knees were
knockin' together like hammers. Was there somep'n like
a can of 'soup' at the end of that fire line? Down there,
mebbe?" He pointed at the floor.

"Perhaps. Wait, though," whispered Jigger. He tiptoed
forward, and snapped on the pencil flash he always carried.

A second door, this one of green enamel over steel,

confronted him. There was a lever in place of a knob, but he did not touch it. Instead, he stepped back.

"We'll leave it as it is for the time being. There might be another fuse there," he said, and bent to examine the floor where the fuse line had gone.

This arrangement was simple but deadly. A tunnel floor tile through which the hole had been bored could be pried out completely. This allowed a man to lower himself four feet. He then was on top of the house sewer leading to the grease-trap under the bricks of the "lawn."

"Let me take the flash, Jigger," Connor whispered. "It slants up under the lab floor, and there are boxes crammed in there. I'd like to take off the detonator first, though...."

A fulminate of mercury cap at the end of the fuse, one open box of sixty per cent dynamite, and three full but unopened cases of the same, came out of that slanting hole.

"Probably intended to blow the place sky-high, if they didn't get the manuals," said Connor.

"Or do it anyway," said Jigger grimly. He backed out of the tunnel, closed the narrow door. They carried over two of the zinc-topped tables to bolster it shut. "They are at the other end of that tunnel," Masters said. "In the house next door. As soon as our period of grace is up we can attack. It's a desperate chance we'll have to take—that we can get to them before they kill Miss Ingalls. God!—what time is it?"

"A little after seven," said Connor.

"Twenty-nine hours to search," Masters said. "They'll rely on that fuse arrangement, thinking that if we find a way into the next house by way of the tunnel we'll blow ourselves to smithereens, and the Brick Wart too, and they could make their escape. Now we'll be able to make a surprise attack. But the damnable part is, even a surprise attack would give them time to murder Miss Ingalls. Where, oh, where, in the name of God are those manuals?"

GAUNT OF FACE from long-continued concentration and strain, Masters drank cups of black coffee each hour. The day had passed, the second night. It was morning of the fateful day. He had been over the entire house now, even the second floor, and he and Gildersleeve were making their second inspection of Seth Bryson's suite on the first floor. If not in the laboratories below, which now Masters felt sure could be written off the books, then the hiding place of the manuals surely *ought* to be somewhere here. Seth Bryson would have been inhuman if he had cached them where he could not put his own hands on them instantly. Then *where…?*

On the table of the hidden cell which adjoined Seth Bryson's bedroom was a large book of photographs. These were temples, art shops of the Orient, a few unskillful close-up photographs of Chinese and Japanese coolies, beggars, priests and merchants. There were streets in some city, probably Peiping.

"Made them himself," commented the detective. "And there's his camera."

He lifted down a large sole leather carrying case, beside which lay a cylindrical tripod case, also in black leather. These had been examined by the police, of course, but Masters opened both and drew out the tripod. There was nothing else in the leather cylinder, no possible place for the manuals.

Masters' heart gave a thump as he lifted out the 4x5 camera. This was a big, expensive box, equipped to use roll film as well as packs and dry plates. In a compartment beside the camera were three roll films still in their yellow cardboard cartons, with tinfoil wrapping outside the black paper on the spindles, and two fresh film packs besides one inside the packholder. On the latter the tabs showed that five of the twelve films had been exposed.

Masters opened the camera, taking out the ground glass screen. The bellows shrouded black interior was empty.

With a scowl he closed and replaced the box in its case. For some unknown reason he had felt a premonitory tingle of expectancy.

"Wonder if he got a snap of one of the noseless men?" Gildersleeve muttered.

Strange, there was nothing in the camera, but just the same Masters hated to let go of it. He started to open it again, but then dropped it in the case and locked the latter. Time was too short to bother about hunches, when once they had been proved wrong. And still he glared back at the camera case.

"Oh, damn everything!" said Jigger, a sudden ferocity in his voice. "I tell you, Gil, I'm stumped. I'm *haunted* by that confounded camera! There's nothing in it, but I keep coming back and coming back to it. Suppose you take a look at the damn thing." He strode out of the room.

So Gildersleeve obediently sat down. Looking for little four-inch rolls of silk, covered with Chinese ideographs, he took the whole camera apart and found—exactly nothing. With a sigh he put the mechanism together again and went to report the failure.

MASTERS WAS FINGERING a tie of brilliant yellow—

the sign he was supposed to give that he had found the manuals.

"I'm going to put it on," he said to Gildersleeve. "If I don't find those accursed things, I'll go out wearing it anyhow. Then you and Milbank and Connor can raid the white house. At twelve. The Death of the Thousand Slices… There is still time to search."

In a state of steadily mounting tension which came to approach a fury, Jigger raced through the whole house again. The hours ticked by—dragging, useless hours for all but him. To him they seemed to fly on the feet of Hermes.

Ten o'clock, and no result. Then eleven… eleven-thirty… twenty minutes to twelve.

"I'm licked," he said hoarsely to Gildersleeve. "Are the police ready to raid? It may mean death for her, but death is certain anyhow. Now that I've failed. Those manuals are here, but I can't find them!"

"All is set," said Gil soberly. "Connor will take the white house, with his squad. Milbank goes through the door down in the basement. He's ready to blast in the tunnel, if necessary. What d'you want us to do?"

"Get a car, and keep me in sight. I'm going to walk around the block wearing the yellow tie and carrying a small parcel. They will think I have succeeded. Somehow I'm going to get to Miss Ingalls. You—follow if you can."

"I'd like to see somep'n stop us," gritted Gil. "I'm carryin' three pineapples latched on my belt."

And that second Jigger stiffened. An expression of amazement swept over his homely visage. He suddenly yelled, "*The films!*" And was darting back inside, making for the cell hideaway next to Seth Bryson's bed chamber.

Inside the hidden room, Jigger Masters grabbed the heavy black camera case, opened it, and snatched out the orange-yellow boxes of roll films. Three of them. Tinfoil covered inside the cartons. Then black paper. These *had* to be the manuals. The spindles of the manuals were said to be four inches long....

A cry of disappointment burst from his taut lips as he rolled off some of the black paper and stared at the first of the three spools. This was not a watered silk manual—but neither was it a new twelve-exposure film!

Tightly rolled underneath five or six thicknesses of the black paper was a thin, tough fiber that looked a little like parchment. On this was English pen-writing in indigo ink!

Not waiting to read any of this queer script, Jigger grabbed up another of the rolls and tore it open.

This time—success! Under the shroud of black showed the coveted silk, covered apparently with tiny, beautifully executed Chinese ideographs in scarlet!

The remaining roll was another manual, the second one!

Seizing the two manuals, he put them in their cartons and them in the side pocket of his jacket. The roll of pen script he took with him, as he ran to find Sergeant Milbank. It would not do to carry this, if it proved to be what he suspected.

"Send this by one of your men right to the D.A.," he commanded breathlessly. "Don't carry it when we close in. I think this is Bryson's story!" And he pressed the third spool into the hands of the astonished sergeant, before sprinting again for the outside door and the spiral way.

The moment Gildersleeve saw him emerge, Gil opened the bronze gate and made for one of the police cars drawn up at the curb. Commandeering this, he drove away, as if to the business section of Hempstead. A block away he turned and came slowly back.

Jigger Masters, wearing the gaudy yellow tie outside his gray tweed jacket, walked slowly—though with a nervous tension in the strides—past the white house with green shutters.

There came no sign from the white house. The noon whistle at Hempstead sounded.

" 'You will be accosted,'" Jigger muttered, quoting the Chinese, Wun Wey. "All right, hurry up and do it." He took the small rolls from his pocket held them aloft. Nothing happened. He dropped his arm, and walked on. They had said to go around the block....

He turned the corner, then stopped, of half a mind to sprint back and demand that the attack upon the white house be launched.

And then came the even hum of a motor. From the east, speeding toward him, came a big car—a Packard! It was the limousine belonging to Seth Bryson. They had come for the manuals. They would release the girl! Even as the car screeched to a sudden stop near him, Jigger noted that a white man in uniform was driving. There were no Chinese in the vehicle that he could see. The chauffeur, pallid of countenance, turned toward him.

"You have a package for—them, Mr. Masters?" he queried, his voice pitched high and unnaturally shrill.

"I have! Where is Miss Ingalls?" said Jigger grimly, strid-ing out straight for the car, and lifting the two precious spools so that the chauffeur could see them.

"She—she's in the back. You c-can lift her out when you

g-give me those," stuttered the man. "D-don't try anything. They've got me covered."

Jigger shoved the two manuals at the man.

At that second the tonneau door swung wide. In there on the floor was a trussed, shrouded figure that had to be Lois Ingalls. And lying down, so they did not appear above the line of windows, one of them holding a blued automatic pistol steadily levelled at Jigger Masters, were two of the masked, noseless monsters!

14

FOR WAYS THAT ARE DARK

THE MOMENT HE bent forward to lift the girl, who was trussed completely, with a sack of some kind over her head, the detective knew that this indeed was Lois Ingalls. She was tall, and, though slender-seeming, was no featherweight to carry.

Also, that second Jigger Masters knew that he had been double-crossed. Breathing fast from his excitement and exertion, he now was conscious of a hellish smell of putridity which filled the car.

With a choked exclamation he straightened, stepping away with the girl in his arms. And at that precise moment the second Chinaman, not the one with the pistol, leaned forward to the car door. He had what looked like a miniature bellows in his hands—a bellows which had a hollow snout of shellacked bamboo....

Compressing the bellows, he drove a thick gray cloud of the putrid-smelling dust squarely into Jigger's mouth and nose. And that was when the Packard, starting with a lurch in second gear, suddenly left the spot and accelerated swiftly, bound west for the corner.

For a moment the detective strangled. He knew full well that this was the breath of the saffron death, and that prob-

ably every one of the tong's victims, from Ralph Marriott to the butler Murphy, had been made to inhale the
lethal dust of zoöspores in this identical fashion! The masks
protected the Chinese murderers from this contamination—the masks that made them seem to be men without
faces.

Doomed—unless Dr. Cortelyou's method proved more
successful than it had in the case of Murphy-Marfowski!

There was no help for it. He glared through watering
eyes, and saw the Packard swing around the corner. And
right then, up rushed the car with Gildersleeve.

"All right, chief?" sang out Gildersleeve. "Shall I chase
'em?"

"No!" Jigger's denial was sharp. Down on his knees he
was jerking off the dirty-looking bag from the head and
shoulders of Lois Ingalls. "Help me!"

He tore away the bag as soon as he could cut the yellow
rope which held it. He stepped away from his wondering
assistant, who immediately set to the task of removing a
handkerchief gag from her mouth, and cutting the other
ropes which held her arms and legs. Jigger Masters shook
the evil-smelling bag.

A cloud of gray dust was left hanging in the air. Dust
which floated slowly down-wind, settling to the ground!
Then he knew Lois had breathed the zoöspores of the
yellow fungus, the eggs of the deadly vegetable that swam!

He swiftly wrapped the death bag tightly in a handkerchief of his own, and handed it to Gildersleeve.

"That's death," he said huskily. "Take it to Cortelyou—
he lives right near the Nassau Hospital. Tell him the saffron
death is in this bag, and that Lois Ingalls has inhaled the

stuff! She must have treatment instantly! He will know what to do. See that the girl gets into the hospital, and is set for the treatment under Cortelyou. If he's not there get Dr. Price, who is in charge of the oscillator, I believe. I'll be over within two hours—if I'm alive when that time comes! I have about that margin for vengeance. The tong inoculated me with the bug, too!"

AT A DEAD run, but gasping because of the smothering load of tiny zoöspores drawn into the air passages of his throat and lungs, Jigger Masters swung back around the corner to Cathedral Avenue.

"We'll attack!" he gasped, motioning imperatively to a motorcycle with armored sidecar in charge of two troopers, which was stationed just off the road behind some shrubbery.

Now the cycle roared into life. Masters made no attempt at secrecy. He shouted to the police who came running from the bronze door of the Brick Wart. Connor with his squad would advance directly upon the white frame house, and Jigger would go with him. In the basement, Sergeant Milbank and the Hempstead police would blast a way through the second tunnel door.

Whistles shrilled. Back in the town of Hempstead somewhere an ominous fire siren whoo-ooed its rising tone of warning. Masters, his pistol drawn, advanced swiftly across the grass.

"A cordon around the house! Two men come with me to the garage. They've backed the Packard into the garage, ready for a getaway...."

From somewhere underfoot came the jarring thunder of an explosion. Milbank had blown out the steel door, the second one which had still guarded the entrance through the tunnel. Immediately then sounded muffled cries, the flat *spat-spat-spat* of exploding automatics fired behind closed doors… then another explosion, probably a grenade….

"Gil will be wild, missing this," thought Masters, on his way to the Packard. "But his job is more important. May the Lord help Lois Ingalls…!"

That was when the automobile leaped toward him and the two Mineola policemen who accompanied him. From one of the windows of the tonneau came puffs of cordite, and the reports of a pistol. One of the policemen crumpled up without a sound, face downward in the driveway.

The attack must have been a complete surprise, since only three of the Chinese—not masked now—were in the back of the limousine. The driver was Claude Gerlach, as before. When he saw the sidecar motorcycle turning to train its Tommy gun, and Masters with the other policeman aiming at him, he screeched in terror and let go of the steering wheel.

That did not save him. The policeman fired straight through the windscreen, catching Gerlach—perfidious or unfortunate as he may have been—full in the chest. He slumped sidewise, dying. The car slowed, lurching in second gear, and started to climb the lawn.

A small, searing agony bit at Jigger Masters' left shoulder, spinning him half around, just as he was about to leap to the running board. He knew he had been hit, painfully but not seriously. Just a hole through the muscle which corded from the base of his neck to the shoulder. His left arm, though, was next to useless.

The tonneau door opened, and a Chinaman clad in blue serge trousers and undershirt leaped out and tried to run. A smoking pistol was in his hand. He raised it to fire again.

Off balance, Masters could not shoot quickly enough. He threw himself sidewise, quick as a cat, and the leaden slug fanned his cheek. Rolling over, grasping, he caught one bare ankle, and tripped the fugitive.

With a snarling screech the tong man kicked, then turned the muzzle of the pistol into his own mouth. There was a shattering report—and one more of the Illustrious Society of Executioners knew more about death.

As Jigger scrambled erect he heard a shrill babble on the other side of the car. The other Mineola policeman had been shot through the knee. In turn he had killed one of the two remaining Chinese. The last one was evidently trying to surrender, though what possible good that might do him was hard to imagine.

Masters sped toward the steps.

The fight inside the white house was bloody but brief. Hemmed in by foes who came at them from the front door, the back door and the cellar of the white house, the four remaining Chinese under Wun Wey retreated stubbornly from room to room, firing back through closed doors— and taking wounds that accounted for two of their number before Milbank's men burst through the last flimsy barrier and slaughtered them like rats.

Masters reached the smoke-filled room just after the last report had died. There were uniformed men on the floor too.

"The headman isn't here!" the detective cried, after a close scrutiny of three dead and one dying Chinese.

"The hell! Is there another one?" ejaculated Milbank. "Berman, Hall, Greene, the top Chink is hiding out. You go and—"

Masters did not wait. The entire downstairs of the house had been invested by police. Likewise the cellar. The detective grimly ran for the staircase leading to the second floor.

WUN WEY HAD not fled. An ancient man, long the American chieftain of a murder society, he himself was both undesirous of defending himself and unable to do so. Once he had seen from the upstairs window that the attackers really had discovered everything, he turned back into the room where Seth Bryson lay stark naked on the bed, scarcely breathing.

Wun Wey took from the sleeves of his brocaded coat the two precious spindles—the film spools on which Seth Bryson had wound the watered silk of the manuals. Dropping the spools so they unwound, rolling away free on the floor, the Chinaman coolly took the two beautifully-colored, curling strips of ideographed silk. He lighted each with a match, and held them in his silver-sheathed fingernails until the last shred had burned. Then he dropped them on the floor and scrubbed the char with his slippers. No one ever again would learn the secret of Ming porcelain from those manuals.

Then from a table he took a tiny-blue jade pipe with a long stem. He filled it with a wisp of tobacco, lighted it, then sat him down in the center of the rug to wait patiently for his fate.

But when there came the sound of hurried footsteps on the stairs he moved again. Laying aside the pipe, he withdrew a small bellows from his sleeve. The hint of a derisive smile in his almond eyes, he puffed out several thick gray clouds into the air of the room. He watched them spread and diffuse through all the chamber, become invisible as they floated into the dampness of the atmosphere.

Then he set the bellows aside quietly, and resumed his pipe.

This was the third chamber Jigger Masters tried. He burst in, pistol ready. He saw the imperturbable, wizened man seated there on the floor, and he stopped. The pistol dropped. Masters sniffed the tainted air. As a last stroke this oldster, resigned to death for himself, intended to take Seth Bryson—doubtless that was the old fellow naked there on the bed—and Masters along into eternity!

"So you are ready to pay the penalty for your sins," said Masters. He hesitated a moment. Then the sounds of other men coming up the stairs decided him. He closed and locked the bedroom door. "It smells of the hellish saffron death in here. I can't let the rest of them breathe it."

"You and I—and that worthless one on the bed—are dead men," asserted Wun Wey. "I have no regrets. To die with one's worst enemy, and also with one's cleverest foe, is no disgrace. I am happy."

"You may not be quite so happy before we're through," snapped Masters. He took Wun Wey under one arm and went to the door.

"Nobody must come in here! The air is death to breathe!" he cautioned. "Here's the chief of the tong, though. Take him, shackle him well, search him for poisons. We want to keep him for the electric chair."

"I shall live only six hours, my son," said Wun Wey placidly.

"Well, we'll see about that. Maybe you're right. Then again, maybe you can learn something from American ingenuity. Take him to Cortelyou," Masters added to the policeman. "Tell Cortelyou that he has been exposed to the saffron death, but that I'd particularly like to have this one saved to pay the legal penalty."

When Wun Wey had been carried down, Masters got Seth Bryson's unconscious form shrouded in blankets and taken to the Nassau Hospital. Bryson would have the same treatment, though from the already palpable faintness of the life flicker in his body there was little hope anything could save him.

At this moment, with siren screaming, a police car drove up and swerved in at the driveway, to curve up part way on the lawn and smash its bumper into the front porch of the house before it could be braked. From it leaped Gildersleeve, frantic because he had been detained so long at the hospital. Masters met him.

"You—you said they'd inoculated *you*, chief!" Gil stammered. "Was that true? You mean you breathed that yellow stuff?"

"Plenty," said Masters in a grim tone. "Did Miss Ingalls get her treatment all right? Yes; well then I suppose I'll be on my way for a dose of the same. Though I don't really put much stock in it, I'll confess. Well, if I have to check in, I'm happy it's at the end of a case like this, not when it is half complete. I'd give something to see that Chinaman executed, though."

"Good God, stop *talking*," wailed Gil. "Every minute is precious. Jump in there. I'll drive you!"

And Jigger Masters, his head reeling from the steady

loss of blood from his torn shoulder, but giving no outward sign now of the deadly saprophytes that swam in his blood-stream, was rushed to the hospital.

15

RADIO FEVER

WILD EXCITEMENT REIGNED in the hospital.

Dr. Cortelyou had Wun Wey in front of the radio fever machine now, the mysterious currents flowing directly through his wizened body. The Oriental it was who calmly asked for an explanation of this mummery. He was positive that he would die in a short space of hours, so why bother? Wun Wey hardly noticed the shackles on his wrists and ankles.

"I'm saving your accursed hide so it can be fried in an orthodox manner!" snapped the doctor vindictively. Cortelyou himself, though keeping out of direct line of the vibrations, felt that half-tipsy elation which goes with the fever.

"You think you can stop the yellow death?" queried Wun Wey with mild derision.

"Wait and see," snapped Cortelyou. "I wouldn't mind failing with you. It came too late for your victim, Seth Bryson."

The old millionaire had expired—from apoplexy, not from the saffron horror—as he was being prepared for the radio treatment.

"The big discovery of what a blessing fever is," the doctor said to the Chinaman, "was made by a Viennese psyciatrist named Wagner-Jauregg, some years ago. Wagner-Jauregg found out that if you gave malaria—paroxysms of high fever, that is—to doomed sufferers from general paralysis, *some* of the sick men and women recovered! Before that time not a single man or woman in the world *ever* had got well of general paralysis through medical treatment! And fever of any desired degree can be induced in a well man by using this machine you see here."

"Now, Miss Tompkins, this patient has had enough. You can wheel him away, and see to it that he is guarded. Then you'd better lie down yourself and cool off. Drink plenty water...."

"And then tell Dr. Price that I'm ready for our other patient, Mr. Masters. I don't dare delay any longer with him. His blood test is worse than that of either of these others...."

So it was that fifteen minutes later, when he had been lying for eight minutes in front of the oscillator, Jigger Masters moved restlessly and opened his eyes. The warmth of artificial fever was mounting in his blood. It was pleasant. But his shoulder ached and throbbed like an ulcerated tooth. And the ache of a worry in his brain now was intensified, too. What had happened to Lois!

He tried to spring from the wheeled cot, but Cortelyou restrained him. Rather hectic words, meant to be soothing, came from the medical examiner, who now was in the direct blast of the ether waves.

Jigger interrupted. He was willing to have the treatment of course; but had Lois Ingalls responded? Was she going to live, or had the horrible saffron death crept further into her veins and arteries? This was all he cared about now.

"I'm betting three to one I'll save you all!" answered Cortelyou jubilantly. Too jubilantly by far. Dr. Price, who entered the room at this moment, stared coldly and suspiciously at his colleague, who was just stating with emphasis: "Your young lady will *live!*"

"You'd better go and pour a pitcher of ice water on your head, Cortelyou!" Price advised. "I'll watch this man. We have a splendid reason to hope, in each of these cases— yours included, Mr. Masters."

AT THE END of half an hour Cortelyou came to wheel Jigger out into a room of his own. For several minutes he stayed, watching closely the rapid drop in temperature. Then:

"You'll have another treatment in an hour, and a blood test in twenty minutes. Get up. You're okay—and there's someone down the corridor I faintly suspect you'd like to see. Miss Ingalls has asked for you a number of times…" Dr. Cortelyou coughed dryly behind his hand, masking a smile. "But hadn't you better wait to put on a shirt, my dear man?"

When Jigger was fully dressed again and completely cooled down as far as the radio fever was concerned, Cortelyou knocked on a door down the hall and entered. With a glad cry Lois Ingalls rose to greet the detective.

"Hm," observed the medical examiner to the bare walls and ceiling. "The radio treatment does just one thing. It heats the blood, making it move swiftly in the arteries. I don't see why another agent which does the same thing should not be beneficial."

And with that he left the room, silently closing the door.

With his first real look at the girl, who stood wistfully

lovely there before him, Masters knew his instinct had
been unerring. Tall, slender, full-breasted, now a little
dishevelled of hair from her experiences in the hospital,
Lois Ingalls could not have managed through long plan-
ning and artistry an appearance more certain to make a
fierce hunger for her urge up in the man.

Without speaking, he went straight to her and took her
in his arms. Then he raised her face a little with one hand
and kissed her fairly on the lips. She did not resist, though
a strange little shiver seemed to agitate her.

"I would never have excused myself—in hell—if I hadn't
done *that*, as long as I was let live to see you!" he said
huskily. "Now do you want me to apologize? I just feel—"

She sighed, half closing her blue eyes.

"No, don't apologize," she answered softly. "Do it
again...."

16

THE SECRET OF THE MANUALS

THE ONLY ONE of three patients taking the radio fever treatment to be ill was the tong chieftain, Wun Wey. His complaint was frustration. He raged inwardly at the knowledge that he and his victims all were getting well. He craftily tried suicide, but failed. They expected just that. Then a strange wideness came to his almond eyes. He, the greatest of all men on earth, actually faced the humiliation of a common death in this plebeian contrivance up at the prison called Sing Sing.

Lois Ingalls and Jigger Masters were happy—more than a little awed and unbelieving, still. But the hospital attaches vied in presenting them with opportunities of being alone with each other; and since both were able to be up and dressed, free except during the times of their radio treatments and blood tests, they reached a firm basis of understanding.

The second day Masters, still a trifle weak from his blood loss, was sitting in a deck chair on the hospital's third floor sun porch, Lois in another chair beside him, when Gildersleeve was admitted. Gil had with him a paper which he had discovered back in the white house of the tong. It read:

My dear Lois:

When this is read I shall have been killed. Of course the police will want to develop these films, so they are bound to come upon my long-guarded secret.

My property goes to you, Lois Ingalls, as to my best knowledge I have no other close relations left on earth. Besides, you have been loyal and kind to an old codger whose springs of loving-kindness had been pretty well dried up before you met him. You will find my will in my vault box at the National City Bank.

Brick-making was my means to fortune. I found myself unable to be content with the mere piling up of dollars, though. So I began to experiment on new sorts of brick, then tile, finally pottery of all sorts and descriptions. I found most of it absurdly easy.

Month by month my appetite grew. I stole one precious secret, and made in my own cellar laboratory a perfect imitation of blue Multan tile.

And of course all the non-secret tiles. Then I turned my hand to "antique" pottery. It became a game with me, fooling the experts. Well, I fooled 'em! I have sold over a million dollars' worth of various sorts of fictile art, supposedly antique, using as my agents some Japanese headed by a fellow named Ichiara Kagodi.

Now I say, let that pottery be considered antique. Why worry the experts who have passed their judgment? I never have spent a penny of the money received for my fakes, but have passed it along to the American Red Cross; If your conscience worries you, dear girl, ask them about the contributions made during the past ten years by a red-head named Maher, an Irishman who was supposed to live right next door....

Of course I was Maher. My only confidant was Claude Gerlach, whom I am leaving $50,000 for his loyal service.

Ming porcelain stumped me. Then, in China, I found out a curious fact. A certain society was "discovering" some of this antique work every year! No one in the world (supposedly) knew how the beautiful blue underglaze and the delicate crackle in Ming was ever secured. But this society knew! In fact, they were manufacturing spurious antiques, exactly as I had been doing with easier kinds, and selling them to collectors for the sake of the great profit.

Well, I managed to bribe a minor priest—poor fellow, he paid for that theft with his life. Then I too knew how to make Ming porcelain! But the Tao Tong tracked me here.

The whole secret lies in the use of an aqueous solution of decaying seaweed in which has been placed millions, yea billions of tiny zoöspores of what I call banner fungus. I got some of this fungus, which grows in fresh water in the American tropics.

When the porous clay has been shaped, it is soaked a day in this solution. Then it is dried and glazed (the Mings used no regular engobe coat, of course), and burned. The fire killed the organisms, naturally. But in hardening they broke down. This made the mysterious blue underglaze (not yellow as some might think, looking at growths of this loathsome fungus), and also gave that network of tiny cracks that is specifically characteristic of Ming and no other porcelain.

That is all, dear Lois. I regret nothing—not even the fact that I am dead as you read this. All happiness to you. You take after my dear sister. Love,

SETH BRYSON.

"Poor Gerlach!" said Lois. Her blue eyes were moist. "Why did he turn against Granddad at the last?"

"I don't think now that he did," said Masters.

"Now, Jigger," said Gildersleeve, "I wonder if you're up to tellin' the boys all about it? The D.A. an' the reporters have been foamin' at the mouth.

"The doc told 'em your blood tests are negative now— yours an' the young lady's. So—"

"Might as well have it over then," nodded Masters. "We'll come out in just a minute or two." He smiled at Lois Ingalls, and Gildersleeve vanished, grinning.

"The Illustrious Society of Executioners," Masters explained, "ran dynasties of emperors. They used manda- rins, governors and other officials just as tools, killing them if they dared disobey. The society was rolling in wealth— up to 1912, when it was mostly destroyed at the time the republic was formed.

"But it did not quite die. In Peiping it was kept alive. Then it invented another way of insuring itself a huge yearly income. It enslaved a number of fictile artisans, and forced them to devote their talents to the manufacture of fake antiques.

"When you stop to think that a man like Ralph Marri- ott paid three hundred thousand dollars just for fifteen pieces—most of them small—of Ming porcelain made by these artisans, you can see how the business was profitable.

"The reason why it brought such a tremendous price lay in the fact that everyone supposed the process for making it was a lost art. But the tong, which by now had a sales branch in America, and probably one in Europe too, made Ming. They used the formula described in two ancient manuals of watered silk, which have been destroyed by Wun Wey."

Masters detailed the process, as he interpreted it from Seth Bryson's pen-written message.

"When the manuals were stolen, and Seth Bryson got away with them and started to turn out Ming porcelain and sell it, the tong probably had a spasm of rage. They swore to get back the manuals, and also to smash every bit which had been made and sold by Seth Bryson.

"That is why they visited the home of Ralph Marriott. The same thing with Josiah Tomeroy. Their deaths were necessary, because the collectors knew that Chinese were concerned in the smashing of Mings.

"The Chinese used as a murder instrument the very spores of the fungus which Seth Bryson and they themselves used in the manufacture of Mings!

"And I may add that I doubt very much that Seth Bryson ever knew this fact about the zoöspores of the banner fungus—that when breathed in the dry or slightly dampened state they invaded the bloodstream of a man and killed him quickly. Else Bryson surely would have cautioned his granddaughter, whom he loved."

"May I interrupt a moment?" asked Casimir Sterling, the district attorney. "I wish you'd make it a little plainer about those—those zoöspores! Some of us, I'm sure, are a little weak in our zoology."

"Zoöspores are plants, not animals," replied Masters. "While not precisely accurate, I've called them vegetables that swim. In reality they are similar to the eggs of hens, or of turtles, in that they develop into duplicates of the parent organism.

"Where they differ lies in the fact that zoöspores *swim!* They have cilia—hairs that act like fins. They swim around until they find a spot that suits them. Then they anchor, and grow fast into the banner fungus.

"This fungus is what stuffed our stuffed men—but I need not dwell longer on that. They showed themselves—the zoöspores, I mean—as a fine gray dust which the Chinese puffed at a victim from a small bellows, or merely put into a bag which they bound over a victim's head.

"This was unlikely to be discovered, as the victim recovered from assault, and did not die until some hours after he had become apparently all right again.

"We can only surmise what happened to Bryson. He was an old man. Doubtless the Chinese began to terrorize or torture him, when suddenly he had a bad stroke of apoplexy. The doctors tell me that was the cause of his death."

WEEKS HAD FLED. The funerals of all who had died because of the Tao Tong were long over. So was the brief and speedy trial at which Wun Wey placidly pleaded guilty. He had recovered his poise; and even the fact that each attempt he made at suicide was balked no longer disturbed his serenity.

There came a midnight when Marsh Vandervoort, with Dorothy, drove his new four-seater amphibian over the smooth waters of Long Island Sound, and mounted into the air, heading northwest. In the double cockpit ahead of Marsh and his wife were Jigger Masters and Lois Ingalls.

"There is apt to be something terrific happen!" Marsh had told them almost in a whisper. "They say there are *thou-*

sands of Chinese who have made it a sort of pilgrimage! They are there now around Ossining, waiting...."

"They will do nothing," said Jigger. "But I'd like to be there."

He had asked Lois to go on this strange midnight journey. Wonderingly she consented. Now they flew west, picked up the dark line of Hudson River, and then went on north.

"The execution is at four o'clock," Marsh told them. "We'll go on up to Albany or further, then circle back to be at Ossining exactly at four...."

On the way north they saw the shadowy prison, and its lights. The big amphibian snored on upriver, then took a wide circle over the Berkshires. Marsh calculated it so that when they came in sight again of Sing Sing a red glow had appeared in the east, heralding the dawn. The hands of his watch showed the time at three minutes to four....

He cut the motor, and instantly there was no sound at all save the singing of the air past the struts of the gliding monoplane.

"Look! Look! The Chinese!" suddenly cried Lois, pointing downward.

There, not far from the walls of the lighted prison, they saw the massed crowd. It was silent, motionless....

Lower and lower glided the amphibian. The four occupants held their breath now. One minute of four... half a minute....

Then suddenly from below rose a murmuring wail of many voices. The Chinese assembled there bowed, each with his forehead to the pavement, while they all mourned the passing of a chieftain of murderers!

Jigger Masters reached out his arm and drew the girl close to him.

"You have seen it all now, all the terrible life I lead. Will you share it?"

"Unconditionally—forever!" she whispered.

THE GOLDEN BULLET

*Frank Crosetti Gulped, Caught at His
Throat, and Went Down in a Twitching
Heap, While Jigger Masters Sat Beside Him,
Powerless to Fend Off the Awful Death*

1

A FRIEND OF IVAN TORK

FOR THE TENTH or dozenth time Jigger Masters shook his head over the contrast. Dr. Ivan Tork had gone into his perfectly kept and spotless laboratory, to phone. As always, going and coming from the laboratory, he carefully locked the door. And out in the living room, where the detective was left to entertain himself, there was an unmade bed, a pile of odorous clothing thrown in a heap on the floor, and a profusion of dirty dishes on the center table.

Outside his laboratory, which occupied the largest room of this basement apartment, the great chemist, Dr. Ivan Tork, lived like a bachelor hog.

Now the key grated. The tall detective smudged out his cigarette with a gesture of impatience. His hazel eyes were watchful as he saw the hunchback chemist emerge from the laboratory, change the door key from inside to outside, and lock the door again.

"I can't refuse to do my best for any friend of yours," said Jigger Masters, rising to his feet. "But all these precautions, Dr. Tork, make me suspicious of my new client. You have helped the law several times with your brilliant analyses. But—I suppose you know that I can't take any client—not

*Jigger Masters stiffened at
sight of a shadowy figure back
of that lettered window.*

even as a return favor to you—who wants me to break the
law?"

"Umph," grunted the hunchback. "All he wants you to
do is save his life. You sought it one time, but did not get
a conviction."

Jigger Masters straightened, and a grim twist came to
the corners of his wide mouth. Frank Crosetti, of course.
Gambler, gunman, killer. There had been a time when the
detective's perfect chain of evidence pointing to Frank
Crosetti as a murderer, had been nullified by three hung
juries afraid of their own lives. After the third trial the case
had been dropped. It was the only exasperating failure on
the record of Jigger Masters.

A slow triple knock at the door.

"He is here," said Dr. Tork unemotionally. "I have discharged my duty. I shall leave you together."

Still collarless and unshaved, the chemist donned jacket and raincoat, then adjusted a round-topped derby on his enormous head. He opened the door, nodded once to the lithe, dandified figure who entered, and left the apartment, closing the door.

The newcomer smiled, bowing from the hips. "I am very glad you could come, Mr. Masters," he said in his adenoidal voice.

"I would not have come if I had known you would be here!" said the detective bluntly. "I don't like you for sour apples, Frank Crosetti!"

"Your dislike is unrequited," smiled the gunman. "I admire you greatly. I will be brief, however." He reached his left hand into the breast pocket of his jacket, withdrew a slim sheaf of yellow-backed bills, and placed them on the edge of the center table. "There is ten thousand dollars," he continued. "It is a retainer. And here is your case. It is really simple. All you have to do is keep me from being murdered."

He handed a single sheet of paper directly to Masters, who accepted it with reluctance. Frowning, he saw that it was the hardest sort of message to trace; each word had been clipped from the eighteen-point subheads of some tabloid paper. Each separate word had been pasted on the sheet:

YOU ARE THE ONLY WICKEDER MAN IN THE WORLD THAN MYSELF. SO I AM GOING TO KILL YOU. PREPARE!

"So there is someone in New York who really feels he is your rival, is there?" asked Jigger dryly, "Does he use golden bullets, too?"

"I do not know," said Frank Crosetti, his careful English the only factor which betrayed his Italian birth. "But you will prevent him murdering me? All I ask is that you find out his name and tell me."

"And you and your golden bullet gang will take care of the rest, eh? I don't like that. I'll be frank with you, Crosetti. I'd much rather be called in somewhat later, and then convict this aspiring wicked man."

"After I'm dead, you mean?"

"Exactly. But because Dr. Tork asks, I cannot refuse to take this sort of case. Just why does a man like Tork feel grateful or obligated to you?"

THE GANGSTER SHRUGGED, smiling easily. "Once I did him a great favor—took a load from his shoulders on to mine. That is an old secret between us, however. I cannot explain further. It has nothing to do with this threat. I feel that this one who envies me, and wishes to see me dead, is not a person of the underworld—or at least does not belong to my part of it. So I prefer to employ a specialist like yourself. When you have discovered the identity of this letter-writer, you may name your own fee, of course."

"This will be plenty. In fact, after I have taken a look over the ground, I may return it. But sit down—if you can find a place in this litter. Tell me briefly when and how you got this warning. Is there anyone at all whom you suspect?"

The gunman nodded and obeyed.

"There are so many really wickeder men in this city," he answered with conviction, "that I have no choice. I am only a killer, you see. No, I suspect nobody; and that is why I am afraid. That letter came by the ordinary mail this morning, and reached me at the Hotel Beaumont, where I live. I got it from the desk clerk at nine o'clock. That is all I know."

With a swift gesture of his left hand he clicked open and proffered a gold-and-platinum cigarette case. Within were *cigos,* tan colored, expensive smokes made of Shiraz tobacco from Persia, with tips of the leaves used as wrappers instead of cigarette papers.

Masters shook his head, and lighted one of his own inexpensive smokes. Crosetti had delayed lighting his *cigo.* Now he *snicked* open a lighter and applied the flame to the *cigo.*

He inhaled deeply. At the same instant he staggered. A gulping sound burst from his throat. He caught at the table for support, spilling the sheaf of thousand-dollar bills.

"Oh, my God!" he croaked in a horrible voice. "Got— *me!"* And he went down in a twitching, convulsing heap on the dirty brown rug.

Masters knelt, and swiftly turned Crosetti to his back, dragging him over under the hanging light. One glance at the eyes, turning up and back, and two quick tests for heartbeat and breathing, and the detective shook his head.

The tan-colored cigo lay there where it had fallen from Crosetti's hand. Masters picked it up gingerly, quenched its fire with a single drop of water from the lavatory tap, and laid it carefully aside on a desk blotter.

There came a sharp rap at the apartment door. Taking out his own pistol and notching up the safety with his thumb, Masters strode to the door, turned the knob, and stepped back. Three business-like, wooden-faced men stood there with hands in the side pockets of their jackets.

A twisted smile came to the detective's lips.

"Come in, gentlemen," he bade in an ironic voice. "Mr. Crosetti is here. I—have just decided to take his case!"

2

─

POISON UNKNOWN

KNOWING THAT THE following hundred seconds would tell whether or not he would continue to live, Masters showed the trio of gunmen the dead body of their leader.

"We hadn't reached a final agreement; but of course this changes everything. It was one of those *cigos* he was carrying that killed him. No, leave them there in his case. The police will have to take charge here. Just so people won't believe I did him in myself—it's common knowledge that I hated Crosetti, after that last trial—it's up to me to get his killer. You can take his ten grand away with you."

The three shook their heads. "Bad luck," said one dryly. "It's your jack. Earn it. Nemmind the flatties. Just tell us who done it. A plain cupronickel slug kills just as dead as an electric singe-and-curl."

"What the hell, Monte?" growled one of the others. "We gonna let this patsy get away with it?" Yellow eyes like those of an alley cat glared at Jigger, who had thrust away his pistol. "There was just him and the boss—"

"And Masters didn't know who he was going to meet," snapped the original speaker. "No, the same guy got Frank who wrote that letter. C'mon now, behave!"

Masters turned his back, and picked up the phone.

Calling Centre Street, he gave his own name, and then
persisted until he was put through to Detective Division
C, where Captain Theodore Haight was to be found at
the moment. Masters and the scrappy captain had worked
together on one previous metropolitan case.

Haight's voice, always brusque, rattled and crashed in
the receiver which Masters held an inch from his ear.

"The devil you say! Crosetti—dead! And *poisoned,* you
think, right when he was talking to you? I'll be right over,
with the doc, the finger-printers and photographers, and
a squad. I don't get what you said about a warning letter,
but never mind till I get there. No use sending out a radio
alarm, you say?"

"None," said Masters, and hung up the receiver.

One of the three gunmen, who had been leaning close to
make sure that this call actually had gone through to police
headquarters, made a sign to his two companions. The
three nodded curtly to Masters, and took their departure.
The sheaf of big bills lay on the floor beside the limp figure
of Frank Crosetti. Masters left it there for the time being.

ONE ODD FACT that harked back directly to the time
when Jigger Masters was trying to get Frank Crosetti elec-
trocuted for murder, came to life as soon as Captain Haight
and his men arrived. The dead man had two beautifully
engraved automatic pistols, both made of solid 18-carat
gold; and both were loaded with special cartridges firing
golden slugs!

One of the two hand-made guns—the one which
had been Frank Crosetti's only talking point in his own
defense—still remained virgin and unfired. The second
one, of course, had accounted for all of his twelve or more

human victims. The fact that Jigger Masters only suspected the existence of this second gun, never getting hold of it for incontrovertible proof, had allowed the suave, sinister Italian to continue his career of murder.

"Well, that makes it all clear enough," said Haight grimly. "Too damn bad you didn't find this gun, Jigger. Beautiful things, aren't they?" He laid them side by side on the table. "Those two gunsmiths discharged from the Sprackling Arms Company, made one—and no doubt made the other."

Medical Examiner Merk arose from his place beside the body, dusting his palms together. "Poison, just as you thought," he said. "No smell, though. Otherwise I'd call it cyanide. We'll have to do some close work on the lungs."

"Unless more than one of those *cigos* was poisoned," pointed out Masters, motioning at the gold-and-platinum case. "Anyhow, this one he was smoking, ought to show." He gestured toward the quenched cylinder of tobacco, resting on the blotter.

A clicking tap of fingernails on the door announced a newcomer to the basement apartment. A squad man opened, and then came over to Haight.

"Sure, let him in," nodded the captain. "It's Dr. Tork. We'll want to ask him a whole lot of questions. Damn funny, bringing you and Crosetti here—and then Crosetti dying of poison. In the dug-out of the greatest authority on poisons—"

He broke off, staring without friendship toward the hunchback scientist who had been for three years the court of last resort in matters of toxicology for the New York police department.

Ivan Tork was an unlovely specimen. His gray hair strag-
gled. His unshaved cheeks showed a white growth of thin
beard. The teeth that showed when he opened his purse-
like mouth, were broken and yellowed. His short arms
moved queerly when he walked, quite as though they were
independent of the long legs below.

"A-ah!" he said throatily, looking down at the corpse
which stretcher men were preparing to take away.

Then his black eyes turned for an instant upon Jigger
Masters in an opaque stare. Then he shook in a silent
chuckle.

"It couldn't be dot *you* were the one who t'reatened him?
Ah, no, dat would be too rich—when he make me ask you
to safe him!"

Dead silence fell, as the medical examiner, Captain
Haight, and the photographers, turned to look queerly at
Masters. The detective shook his head slowly.

"We'll table that suspicion for the time being," he said
dryly. "I want to ask one thing, Dr. Tork. What was the
favor Frank Crosetti once did for you—the burden he took
from your shoulders on to his own?"

"Favor?" Tork looked puzzled. Then his big head shook
once sidewise in jerky fashion. "Oh, you mean not shoot-
ing me, when I get you here to meet him? Dat is the only
favor—if you call it dat. I did not want to die—so-o-o." His
short arms came out expressively, palms upward.

"And you didn't know Crosetti? Never had any previous
dealings with him at all?" persisted Masters, his hazel eyes
holding level on the face of the scientist.

"Neffer!" said Tork, almost contemptuously. "I care for

no man. Unless that man come to me and say, 'Do this or you die.' Then—perhaps—I maybe do it!"

The body was carried out then, and the medical examiner took charge of the partly burned *cigo* Crosetti had started to smoke. He would send this to Hegemann, the city analyst.

Masters and Haight looked at the remaining contents of the gold-and-platinum case.

"See here—and here?" said Masters, pointing at two more of the eight remaining *cigos*. A tiny brown stain appeared on the two indicated, near the tip of each. This had to be the end the smoker lighted, since the *cigos* were tipped in gold leaf.

"I have a hunch," said Masters in a grave voice. "This is the fastest-acting poison I've ever encountered or heard about. Even faster than pure cyanogen gas! I'd like to take one of these brown-marked *cigos* and have our friend Tork here analyze it. Hegemann is good in his field. But if this is some new poison, or a new concentration of some old one, he's apt to miss. Tork won't."

Haight assented to this, and the chemist, shrugging, said he would do the analysis. "It is probably someding easy enough, and your Dr. Hegemann will find it. But because it happens here in my place, I am interested. I will let you know tomorrow." He took one of the tan *cigos* with the dark brown mark near the tip, and carried it into his laboratory, locking the door behind him.

"If they put a human brain in a wart-hog, they'd have—him!" said Haight, jerking a thumb toward the closed door. "This is going to be a hell of a case, Jigger. The papers are going to do more nasty hinting even than usual. Here I've got a celebrated dead man, dead of some fancy poison. Dead in the home of N.Y.U.'s famous research toxicologist—and dying in the presence of J.C.K. Masters, the private detective who hated Frank Crosetti... by the way, *did* you hate him that much, Jigger?"

"No, I didn't kill him; but I think I know who did," said Masters quietly.

"You mean—Tork?"

THE HAZEL EYES smiled coldly. "I think we'll find that Crosetti actually did seek out Tork, knowing I'd been down here with three-four analyses. It would be a way to get me in on a case that would appeal to a wire-puller like our golden gun specialist. I could scarcely refuse Tork, particularly if he said his own life hung in the balance. And, knowing Crosetti, I've no doubt it did."

Haight frowned. "Well, I suppose you're in this up to the ears," he said. "Tell me when you get something definite, though, won't you?"

"Naturally," nodded Masters. "Now, let me have one of those unmarked *cigos*. I've got an odd notion there may not be many of them made or smoked."

A moment later he took his departure, emerging to the chill night air of Seventy-seventh Street, walking to the subway station at Seventy-second Street and Broadway, and there catching a train for Brooklyn.

Out in Flatbush lived a man, an Armenian wholesaler of tobaccos, who would know everything about *cigos*.

Masters was in luck. Ferd Kalenderian was in the bosom of his family, and delighted to have a visit from his good friend, Jigger Masters. The old Armenian was a shade too obsequious and anxious to be of service, bowing incessantly and smoothing his long, silky beard. The detective knew, however, that this was only the heritage of many generations of fearing Turkish officialdom in the old country. Kalenderian began to quiver inwardly whenever authority of any kind spoke to him.

The tobacco importer recognized the *cigo* at a glance.

"O-o-ahh!" he exclaimed raucously, as though clearing his throat. "That is Shiraz. A fine tobacco. From $2.25 to $2.50 a pound wholesale in America. Not used so much, you understand. And yess-s, the *cigo!*

"There is only one man in New York who makes them all the time. Only one, I am quite sure. They must cost too much, you know. Fifty cents for ten, made with gold tips, like this."

"All right, Ferd. What's his name?" nodded Masters. "I just want to ask him a question or two about a client of his."

The tobacco importer was willing enough to furnish the information. Five minutes later Masters was walking to the subway again, bound back to the east side of Manhattan. An address on the north side of Twentyseventh Street, between Lexington and Third. There a countryman of Ferd Kalenderian's, Nahigian by name, lived and had his *cigo* factory in a loft....

On the ride Masters searched back through memory. There had been an angry, vengeful woman once in Crosetti's life—a woman he had divorced for cause, but who swore in court she had been framed. She had married again—and still a third time, following another divorce which she herself obtained. Masters could not recall her last husband or his name.

"If this *cigo* maker has a woman customer, it will be time

to check," he reflected. "She would know his vanities and his habits—all except the secret of the golden gun. She was a sort of divorce racketeer. Crosetti probably did frame her, thereby beating her to the punch...."

It was one o'clock in the morning when Masters reached the address on Twenty-seventh, and the second floor factory windows were dark. At one side there was a locked door at sidewalk level, but no bell or knocker. In vain the detective hammered on the door for several minutes, and even kicked it with the sole of his shoe. No one answered.

Frowning, he backed out into the almost deserted street, looking upward. Four dirty windows were there, one of them bearing the legend:

V.E. NAHIGIAN
TOBACCOS

That second he stiffened. There was a street light above; and a little to the left of his own head, making certainty difficult; but he could swear that a shadowy figure stood just back of that lettered window, staring down at him!

A man crouched there—or a woman! And there was a black, narrow rectangle cutting across the dim whiteness of the half-seen face. A silk mask?

Catching a stifled breath, Masters stepped quickly back to the sidewalk where he could not be seen from above. There was no conceivable reason why a *cigo*-maker should fail to answer a thunderous knock on his own street door, and then wear a mask in his own locked dwelling. Was it an ordinary burglar?

"My hunch is different!" said Masters grimly to himself.

Two courses were open to him. He could go for help, or he could wait here in the hope that the masked intruder might come out the front way.

3

DEAD MAN ALOFT

"OVER MOST ALL of New York there are no alleys—no back doors," he reflected swiftly. "In these very old tenements, though, I seem to remember a sort of rear court with a common way out to another street...."

Either way was risky. Alone, he might be shot down—perhaps even from that upstairs window—before he had any legitimate reason for drawing a weapon of his own. If he left to seek a policeman on the next corner, or make a hurried phone call, that mysterious masked person might escape.

He made an instant decision. Turning, he sprinted at top speed for Third Avenue. There always were police patrolling the grim, run-down district which clings to the "El" structure.

This time there was no uniform in sight. Hastily then Masters dashed into an all-night lunchroom, dialed Spring 7-3100, and left the brief message with his name. Send a radio car instantly. If Haight could be found, tell him to come also; Masters needed him.

He jammed down the receiver and dashed out, turning the corner. At a steady jog-trot he returned the half block.

Had these six or seven minutes afforded the mysterious intruder time to escape?

Evidence on this point was plain. Instead of being locked or bolted, the stairway door at which he had hammered, now stood open inward. Beyond stretched a flight of worn stairs, vanishing into obscurity above. A nose-tingling smell of dried tobacco hung in the air.

Masters did not mount the stairs. If Captain Haight did not come, the detective was going to have a hard enough time explaining his presence, without being found snooping around a manufacturing loft at quarter after one in the morning.

But he had less than a minute to wait. Around the corner swung a squad car, siren bellowing. It drew up opposite the loft factory, and two uniformed men and a plain-clothes detective leaped out. Haight was not among them; but Masters noted, with a degree of relief, that the plainclothes man was Detective-Sergeant Sam Willis, with whom he had a slight acquaintance. Willis, who came directly to Masters, frowning a little, was an intelligent if somewhat impetuous man.

"Our bird's flown, Sam," said Masters. "Don't know for sure whether it was a woman or a man. I'm not going to try to explain the whole thing right now; but I want you to search that factory loft up there. Nahigian's place. It's the *cigo* factory—a direct hook-up with the killing of Frank Crosetti. And I think there may be something pretty bad up there."

"You haven't been up, Jigger?" asked Willis searchingly.

"No."

"Well, let's take a look-see then," said Willis, and walked

through the doorway. His blue eyes had been grave, noncommittal; and Masters realized full well that on the face of it Sergeant Willis had many reasons for being skeptical of his strange story.

Two doors opened at left and right at the head of the stairs. One was locked. This, they established later, gave into another loft, now unoccupied.

The door to the right stood ajar. They pushed in, warily flashing torches; and immediately one of the policemen sneezed. The air was dead, and heavy with tobacco dust which irritated the nostrils.

"Anybody here?" called Willis, staring about the front room which was evidently the *cigo*-factory. Boxes and bales of tobacco were stacked against one wall. There were three tables on which lay scraps of leaf and shred-cut tobacco, spring-backed chairs on which the makers worked, and a litter of dust, paper and miscellaneous trash on the floor. The room was empty of human occupants.

Willis snapped on a wall button, which lighted three green-shaded drops above the tables.

"Try the back room, boys," he bade, gesturing toward a doorway hung with a faded and villainously dirty green baize curtain on brass rings.

The first man in stopped suddenly with a throaty cry of discovery. Coming swiftly after him, Masters glimpsed a scene of sordid tragedy. Here was a dingy, windowless alcove about twelve feet deep. It held a trunk, a battered chiffonier and a disordered cot. And sprawled from the cot, a blanket still twisted about his legs, lay a fat, short man in a contorted, wholly unnatural position.

Eyes and mouth were wide as if he had been strangled,

but there were no marks on his bare, flabby throat. He had been wearing a union suit in lieu of pyjamas. Masters swiftly bent and unbuttoned this garment in front. There was no sign of bullet or knife wound.

"I think you'll find this similar to Crosetti's case, Willis," said Jigger Masters quietly, rising and dusting his hands. "Poison—but whether or not administered in a *cigo,* is difficult to guess from externals. There's no smell of burned tobacco here; only the stuff in bulk."

"Are you sure he's dead?" demanded Willis. "Sa-ay, *how* are you so damn sure so quick?" His scrutiny of the private detective was far from friendly now. "And how did you happen to be on the scene this way? Why, the fella's still *warm!*"

"Oh, don't waste your time suspecting me," shrugged Masters. "Haight will tell you why I have to be in this case. I went to the home of Ferd Kalenderian, the tobacco importer, found who was the only man in New York to make *cigos,* and came here immediately. You can check that.

"Anyhow, this dead man is doubtless V.E. Nahigian, maker of *cigos.* By the looks of things he had two factory helpers, who went home nights.

"NAHIGIAN PROBABLY WAS alone, asleep, when that killer entered. I can only say I'm sorry I didn't get on the scene ten minutes earlier; but that's the way of it. Now, where is Captain Haight?"

"Probably in bed now—or back at headquarters," responded Willis somewhat sulkily. "There doesn't seem to be any phone here. D'you want to ride with Allison, and send Merk along to look at the body?"

Masters grinned. This fitted into his plans, though he

saw through the subterfuge easily enough. Detective-Sergeant Willis knew too much about some of the sordid business in which private detectives sometimes engaged. The coincidence of Jigger Masters being on the scene of two crimes in one night—and when motive, as well as opportunity, was far from unimaginable—was getting the best of the sergeant's respect for the proved ability and hitherto spotless escutcheon of Masters.

"I'll be glad for a ride to Centre Street," smiled the detective, "And meanwhile you concentrate on finding traces of a woman or a man who has been here buying *cigos* recently. That's the person wanted for two murders."

"Maybe," agreed Willis darkly. "I've got some of my own ideas about that, though!"

Patrolman Allison was a better driver than conversationalist, so the ride down to headquarters was brief and silent. But there Masters was lucky. He found that Haight had just returned, grimly jubilant. He had made a discovery of his own which he would mention in a moment.

"Willis beat it out and phoned, the minute you left. I just talked to him," said Haight, grinning—but with a glint of measuring calculation still in his gray eyes. "He thinks you've bumped another one!"

Haight winked broadly, gesturing to one of his office chairs. "I want to hear all about that, since there's sure to be a link with Crosetti's death. How the hell did you happen to be on the spot—again?"

Masters shrugged away the innuendo, since he was sure Teddy Haight did not really think him a murderer. Briefly he related the short steps which had taken him to Brooklyn, thence to the maker of *cigos* on Twenty-seventh Street.

"Poison is normally a woman's weapon," he said quietly. "The person I saw vaguely up there behind the window might easily have been a woman. I think she or he was masked, too. And a narrow black mask is more what a woman would use."

"The hell!" ejaculated Haight, nettled. "But where do we get a woman in this? Crosetti wasn't much on skirts. He stuck to big-stakes gambling, with a lil murder thrown in once in a while."

"No—but do you remember his wife? He framed her—just about the time she was going to frame him, probably. He got the divorce! I seem to recall that she made some wild threats then. That was seven-eight years ago. Look it up."

"I will," nodded Haight, making a pencil note on a pad. "You almost cut across-lots and got in your kill," he added. "But that miss will put the killer more on her—or his—guard.

"Meanwhile, I have been up to Crosetti's hotel apartment at the Beaumont. He bought those *cigos* by the thousand, from Nahigian, as you say. See here. This is the last box!"

From the wide central drawer of his desk he lifted a beautifully-grained case of Circassian walnut bound in strips of white metal—either silver or platinum. Opening the long, wide box, which evidently had been made for this special purpose, Haight showed five compartments. Four of the five held contents still concealed by coverings of lead foil.

The fifth compartment exactly fitted a light wooden box of a size to accommodate two hundred *cigos*. Perhaps one hundred and seventy-five lay there now, the box being disturbed only at one end. Frank Crosetti evidently had dipped in here to fill his *cigo*-case twice.

"I haven't gone into it thoroughly yet," said Haight, "but see here—and here?" He pointed at the top layer where the tan-colored cylinders had not been disturbed. "Each one has that dark brown dot. None of those below the top layer seems to have it. I believe the poisoner came with a hypo needle, and squirted some of that poison into each *cigo* in the top layer only. I'm going to call Hegemann in a minute, and find out what he thinks it is."

"Glad I didn't take one of Crosetti's smokes when he offered his case to me," grimaced Masters. "And say, by the way, I wish you'd call Dr. Tork and ask him if he has analyzed that poison, too."

"You do that," nodded Haight. "Use this phone. I'm going around to see Hegemann now." The captain arose, and strode out of the office, and Masters lifted the phone receiver.

A moment later he got the snarling, disgruntled voice of Dr. Ivan Tork. Before he asked a question, Masters knew that the chemist had not succeeded as yet in the analysis. A failure of any sort, or even momentary bafflement, made him surly and vindictive.

"No, damn you, Masters!" he roared. "I told you tomorrow! I have not finished yet—and I don't know!" The receiver crashed down at the other end of the line, and Masters shrugged. He lighted a cigarette and leaned back, inhaling deeply.

A minute later Captain Haight strode back with his fast, impatient step. "Hell!" he growled. "Any luck with Tork?

No? Well, it's the same here. Hegemann's up a stump, and says he's going to quit till tomorrow. He's tried all the standard tests, and none of 'em show positive! He was beginning to think that maybe that stuff wasn't poison at all, so he soaked one of those dark brown spots, and injected a cubic centimeter into the office cat—my cat, damn him!"

"Nicotine?" asked Masters laconically.

"Nicotine, hell! There isn't enough nicotine in that whole damn bunch of *cigos* to make a cock-a-lotch dizzy! No, I'm out one prize Persian tom-cat, that's all! Damn German idiot!"

"But you know now that poison *was* there in the *cigos*, and that it killed Crosetti," soothed Masters.

"Yes, I know—and a helluva lot of good that does! *Poison unknown!*"

4

THE WORLD'S WICKEDEST WOMAN

THIS TITLE HAD been given Julie LeGendre, present Marchioness D'Elage, by her own press agent. That had been when she was appearing in vaudeville, following her sensational divorce from Cyril Bingham of Hollywood.

That press agent probably earned his money. It took talent, keeping the public interested—and not disgusted—when a beautiful, if brazen, woman indulged herself in a new marriage on the average of every sixteen months, attaching to herself most of the real and personal property of each ex-husband as she swept along. Breaking a few foolish hearts, no doubt. Causing a suicide or two among the weak men. But because of the press agent, the notorious Julie was always good for a luscious, and revealing photograph (Story on p. 3), and therefore was invaluable to a certain group of tabloid papers.

This noon of the day following Frank Crosetti's murder, the fair, languorous and seductive Julie for the first time in her life looked a perfect thirty-six—in age as well as measurement. The morning papers were rumpled and strewed on both sides of the chaise longue in her boudoir. Clad in topaz-buckled slippers, a diaphanous *robe de nuit* which could have been crushed and drawn through her latest platinum wedding ring, and a startling jet silk garment which wound twice about her body and fastened with a single topaz pin, she had left her breakfast tray on the ottoman, and walked up and down the fussy and luxuriously fad-ridden room.

More than once she parted the curtains and looked down upon the monotonous traffic of the motored snails on Park Avenue; though what she could hope to discern from the sixteenth floor was hard to imagine.

"Marie! Hasn't that poky fool of a detective come yet?" she suddenly cried, addressing the maid who waited silently in the adjoining bedroom.

"No, madame," came the quick, reply. "He tol' me twelve-thirty. It is still five minute'. But listen! Is that heem?"

Brrr—brrrr-brrrrr!

Three rattlesnake buzzes announced a house call from the foyer-desk downstairs. The private detective, J.C.K. Masters, desired to see the Marchioness D'Elage....

It was to prove an exasperating experience for the fair Julie. Jigger Masters, busy since arising from a short sleep, at nine o'clock, had meant to interview this woman—but had no idea in the world that she would have the brazen nerve to demand *his* presence! And he had been a trifle annoyed at the imperious manner in which Julie's maid had sent for him, assuming that he, like practically all males of thirty-odd, would fall all over himself to obey any behest of her mistress.

Now Masters came briskly in, ignored the maid, saw Julie waiting for him in a studied pose on the chaise longue of her boudoir, and grimaced slightly. Breath-taking this woman might seem to some men; but the detective's craggy features gave no sign that he was the least impressed.

"Madame LeGendre?" he asked. "I had been intending to call on you. It was kind of you to ask me. Did you finally carry out your threat and kill Frank Crosetti?"

"Did *I* kill—oh, my God!" gasped Julie. "No, no! Oh, of course not! I—why, I haven't even thought of Frank for— well, for years! No, I wish to employ you to—to stay here and guard me!" she broke in nervously. "I—I, too, have been wicked—and I knew Frank. I need you for a bodyguard!"

Masters shook his head. "Not that," he said. "I am in this case already; but one man can't guard a person against an unknown murderer. There are too many unexplored avenues of approach. It's a job for the police—if for anyone—while I go after the murderer. Even if the police detailed a dozen men to keep you safe, a clever murderer, anxious enough to take the risk, could kill you. Still, they will be far better than I could be."

He walked over and lifted the Continental phone.

"Oh, no! No!" cried Julie, catching his arm, "Not the stupid police! You! I want you to stay near me—"

Masters held her away one-handed, without answering. Getting his connection, he told his story briefly to a desk sergeant, asking that Haight be notified as soon as he arrived, and that, meanwhile, detectives be sent down to Julie's apartment as a guard.

The woman had given up, and now sat on the edge of the chaise longue. Her face showed undoubted pique. This impersonal young man seemed to regard her wishes as of no importance, and Julie was not used to that.

"Is there some man—one of your ex-husbands, or some

other lover—whom you suspect of hating both you and Crosetti?" asked Masters, coldly.

"Why, I suppose it might be—no, there can't be anyone now. I just thought, of course—" A frown of vexation appeared on Julie's forehead. *Why* didn't this private detective act more deferential, more like the hired servant she deemed him?

"So you have nothing at all to tell me? Nothing that might help me catch this killer—before he troubles you?" persisted Masters. "No?" He nodded, a satirical twist to his wide mouth. "Did you wish to bribe me, perhaps?" He gazed at her closely, wondering just what was her game. "Well then, madame, I must leave you to the tender mercies of the police. I hope they take your unexplained fears seriously. I do. I advise you to think over everything, and tell it to them—any suspicion that may arise in your mind. There may be just a crank, bent on believing himself the most wicked man in the world, but I doubt it. The fact that you were once married to Frank Crosetti, and feel that you may be nominated as the second victim, looks far too fishy.

"Think of the various men you have double-crossed. One of them may very well have decided to wipe you out, with all your husbands and admirers! But now I must be going. In case anything definite arises—"

"You mean, if I'm found dead!" suddenly burst out Julie. "*Then* you'll pay some attention! Is that the way a man th-thinks a woman—" She gave way to tears and sobs, artistically, of course.

"Hm," said Masters dryly. "Pardon me if I leave the police to sympathize, madame. I can be of far more use out after the killer, than squeezing your handkerchiefs dry for you. But I'll give you one bit of sound advice, since you are trying to appear really afraid—though for no reason you are ready to admit frankly.

"When Captain Haight or Sergeant Willis gets here, tell him and him alone where you're going. Then dress yourself in something you don't usually wear—something plain. Borrow clothes from your maid, if you can.

"Take absolutely nothing with you. Leave this apartment, your servants, and everything just as it is. Go to some obscure but good hotel, changing cabs on the way. Have Haight send a man to you with cigarettes, cosmetics, liquor—whatever you need, and all newly purchased. Fix yourself up for a week's stay incognito in that hotel room—and *stay* there! By that time I'll surely have the murderer!"

"Oh, but I couldn't do a thing like that!" snapped Julie crossly. "What do you think I am, a—"

She stopped with her mouth unhandsomely open. It was the first time since Julie had been fourteen years old, that any masculine creature had walked out and left her to her own fears and seething displeasure.

HER PRESS AGENT was waiting. She had talked somewhat hysterically to him on the phone; but that high-pressure gentleman was not alarmed. He was wound up tight now with plans for utilizing all this Crosetti publicity, and turning it into munificent vaudeville contracts. Oddly enough Julie herself vetoed his plans for an immediate campaign, featuring her in her old role as "wickedest woman"—as Frank Crosetti had been called the "wickedest man," by the murderer.

"Not now!" she shivered. "It will be all right when—when that awful man is caught. But now, take me out for a ride somewhere. I don't want to be here when the police come. Marie can tell them everything."

Five minutes later they descended in the elevator. Julie clutched the press agent's arm, and stared about apprehensively. No one was in the marble-and-limestone foyer of the expensive apartment save the usual uniformed attendants, and a pair of girls at the switchboard back in the rear. Julie breathed easier, yet kept close to the natty figure of her escort as he went out to ask the doorman to call a taxi.

The doorman bowed, walked to the curb, blew his whistle and held up one hand. From a half block south a yellow cab swerved to the right from the traffic procession, and came to a halt at the curb, the driver reaching sidewise to push down his metal flag.

At that moment, from the next side street, one hundred feet distant, a shabby sedan—a Chevrolet spattered with dried mud—turned north on Park Avenue. It held close to the curb till it neared the waiting cab. Then it angled slightly out.

Julie and the press agent quickly crossed the sidewalk, the man ready to help her into the cab. Julie hesitated, casting one half-furtive glance north, then south along the double boulevard.

At that instant she gasped soundlessly, in terror too great for any movement to save herself. The driver of a shabby-looking car had leaned far to the right, holding his steering wheel momentarily with his left hand. And he was pointing a pistol straight at the petrified Julie!

The tiny sound, no more than would be made by the popping of a wine cork, was lost in the drone of traffic.

Not so Julie's sudden shriek of pain! Staggering back,

half falling into the press agent's arms, she clutched at her left cheek. A thin trickle of red came out from between the exquisitely manicured fingers.

"He shot me!" she screamed, clawing at her cheek. "A man in a Chrevolet—shot me!" Something small and dull-yellow under the film of blood, came away in her fingers. It was a tiny, soft slug of 22-carat gold, the same sort of pellet—though not of the usual lead—manufactured for use in an air pistol toy which can be purchased at any department store.

Pandemonium! The press agent, who had not seen the Chevrolet—and its sinister driver, thought his employer was out of her mind. So, supporting the struggling, frenzied woman, he commanded the doorman to help him carry Julie.

Just then a squad car sailed up, and policemen swarmed out—too late.

They all were a trifle dazed and stupid about it. The wound on Julie's cheek did not look like much. It would scarcely leave a scar. It was only when Detective-Sergeant Willis saw the tiny pellet of gold, that he became alarmed.

And by that time there had come a new, convulsive quality in the woman's frantic struggles. Her screams ceased abruptly. For fifteen seconds then, with only hoarse, formless sounds coming from her arched throat, she shuddered, became rigid, stiffening back, back—until she went limp, spots of white froth in the corners of her mouth.

Julie LeGendre, Marchioness D'Elage, had gone to compare sins with the sirens of another world. And it was not until they knew she was really dead, and unclasped her tightly clenched fingers, that they discovered the note which had caused all her genuine fright and misgivings.

It was similar in content to that which Frank Crosetti had received.

Your wickedness has been of a mean sort. Still, I cannot abide having the world think that even a woman can be as wicked as I know myself to be. Prepare yourself for death!

5

RIGHT ABOUT FACE

ON RETURNING TO Centre Street from Julie's apartment, Masters had tried a second time that morning to get Dr. Ivan Tork on the phone, without success.

"He's missed, too," said Jigger with a grimace. "I'll have to go out there. Any time anything eludes him he sulks like a punished baby. Takes his phone receiver off the hook, and keeps on trying this and that, checking and rechecking his results. It's even hard to get in by knocking, but I've done it."

Captain Haight shook his head wearily. "Hegemann swears this is a new poison," he said. "The regular tests for toxic radicals don't work. And yet it's something terrific. There wasn't more than one-tenth grain in any one of those *cigos*. Hegemann thinks it's some variant of fluorin hooked up to C_2N_2—cyanogen gas."

They launched then into a discussion of the search which had been done on the Crosetti note. The paper and mucilage both were ordinary, and the cut-out words had come from a well-known New York tabloid. There were no fingerprints; no usable clew of any sort.

Then it was that a vastly excited Sergeant Willis arrived with the tiny golden bullet which had killed Julie LeGendre, and the tale of her sudden end. He showed the death note.

"It was poison did it—probably the same poison!" cried Willis. "You think Nahigian was poisoned, too, don't you?"

"Yes, dammit!" growled Haight, getting up and pacing his office. "The killer probably dropped some in his mouth while he lay there snoring. And bingo! Nahigian never really woke up!"

Masters' face was set. It was just possible that he might have seen this killer in time, if he had stayed with Julie. Still, without even guessing that she had this real reason for sudden panic, he had given her the very best advice, and she had disregarded it, leaving her apartment for the public street before the police got there. She had no one but herself to blame.

"I'm going up to Tork's now," he told Haight. "You didn't leave any men there, did you?"

"Hell, no," snapped Haight. "All right. Maybe we can go some place when we know what that poison is. Otherwise—well, I've got men working on Crosetti's past, and now I'll sick 'em on the fair Julie. Trouble is, both of 'em had too many enemies. At least fifty people might have wanted to kill one or the other."

"And one of them did," nodded Masters, leaving the station, a thoughtful frown on his forehead.

Riding north on the subway, then walking from Seventy-second Street, Masters reached the dingy brownstone front where the smelly and squalid basement apartment of the scientist was located. Descending the stairs, Masters wondered again why Tork should have such a place. His laboratory, where he worked usually in preference to the big, perfectly equipped place furnished him by New York University, was immaculate. But the two outside rooms in which he lived his ordinary life, could not have been surpassed for filth and ugliness in the lower East Side itself.

Masters knocked on the door at the bottom of the stairs. After a minute he repeated. There came a rustling from within, and then the sound of a key grating in the lock. The door swung open a foot, revealing a greenish incandescence—one of the doctor's queer tube lights, filled with strange gases of which he alone knew the names.

Tork's shaggy, enormous head appeared at the level of Jigger's shoulder. "Who is it now?" rasped the doctor's unpleasant voice. A smell of gin, added to the heavy reek of chemicals, dirty clothes, stale food and airless living, came through the aperture.

"It's Masters. I came to find out if you had anything on that poison," said the detective. "Hegemann's at a loss." He almost had to push a way into the place, so grudging was Tork's welcome.

"I will haf it—but not yet," snapped Tork. "You are so damn impatient! It is not a simple poison. That I haf found out already. Dere is cyanogen—but not free. Probably it will be some complex compound that is broken up by dilution in blood."

There was a stone jug on the littered table, containing gin; and from this the chemist swashed out a full tumbler, offering it to Masters. The detective shook his head.

"Oh, I make it myself. It is good," snarled Tork. "No poly-aldehydes in this. The liquor sold now is worse than during your damn-fool Prohibition. But den—" The hunchback shrugged, tilted the tumbler, and downed the contents in four swallows, quite as if the acrid liquor had been so much water.

"You tell me some more—about how the poison worked," he gasped, wiping his mouth with the back of a hairy wrist. "It went quick, eh? Painful?"

"Both, I should judge," said Masters. "Crosetti—"

"But was dere not another death? If two people die—"

MASTERS SUDDENLY WENT tight inside. Had the papers mentioned any poison in regard to the death of Nahigian, the *cigo*-maker? There was no chance, of course, that the chemist had heard of Julie LeGendre. No chance at all, unless....

"It isn't proved that the same person killed that *cigo*-maker," he managed to answer indifferently, though his scalp began to prickle. "Anyway, I believe in tackling one thing at a time. The police and I are completely baffled, so far. I want to know about this poison. Then perhaps I can make a guess—as to who may possess such stuff."

Jigger Masters did not take his departure now, though he saw that Dr. Tork expected him to go. He stayed on for several minutes, talking, scarcely knowing the inconsequential things he said. That had been a break on the chemist's part. He at least had some knowledge greater than anything he had told. What could the connection be between him and Crosetti—and Julie LeGendre?

What could be Tork's motive, if he were the killer—or an accessory?

Motive! What *could* it be? Or was this conjecture the merest moonshine? Of a certainty, facts like the ownership of a car could be proved, or quickly disproved. And then, of course, Masters could ascertain just how much about the second murder had crept into the papers prior to his arrival at Tork's place.

At this moment, however, he felt the chilling certainty that not one word had connected the death of Nahigian with that of the gangster, Frank Crosetti!

He became aware that the hunchback was speaking.

"… crate of delicious apples, from a pupil of mine who moved out to Oregon three years ago.…"

A change had come into Dr. Tork's manner. He was staring queerly. His brows, raising while his eyes were slitted shut, lifted the upper lids, exposing the whites in a crescent above the coal black irises.

"… so I'd like to give you a couple or three of dese apples. Too many for me alone. I'd get hyperchlorhydria if I ate them all.…"

He got up, agile enough for all his hump, and the liquor he had consumed. He went out one of the two doors leading from the squalid living room. One of these doors, always kept locked, opened to his immaculate laboratory. The other door…?

Dr. Tork reappeared from that other room a minute later, carrying a small crate of the most magnificent rosy-cheeked apples Jigger Masters had ever seen. Each specimen was as large as a small grapefruit, with the sheepshead shape characteristic of this brand.

"I'll put a few in a bag. Will you eat one now?" queried the chemist, bringing the crate forward for Masters to choose.

"Thanks—only one," the detective managed to say. "I'll eat it while I walk down to the subway."

Was it sheer imagination, or did the hunchback *force* his

choice from a certain row of apples—the way a stage magi-cian makes a dupe select a certain card from the spread deck? Masters gave up, shrugged, and took one. He shined it with his handkerchief, and then rose to his feet.

"I'll call you back about six," he said offhandedly. "I hope we know more about that poison by that time."

The chemist chuckled dryly. "I have no doubt we will," he answered, and closed the door, locking it behind Masters.

The detective found difficulty in breathing, until he had got out of the apartment, turned west on the sidewalk, then sharply south at the next corner. Then he drew up against a wall, took the apple out of his pocket, and scrutinized it sharply.

Cold beads of horror sprang from the pores of his fore-head.

There on the rosy cheek of the fruit, was a tiny brown-black mark—a puncture, with some kind of brownish substance oozing from the minute aperture!

"It is the poison!" cried Jigger Masters in an awful voice.

6

THE WICKEDEST MAN

TWENTY-TWO MINUTES LATER, after some quiet but thrilling words had been spoken over the telephone, Jigger Masters stood again at the foot of the stairs in Tork's basement. For a moment he listened intently, but no sound came from the apartment. Then he took a deep breath, and crouched down on the steps in front of the door, holding his abdomen.

A hollow, heart-rending groan burst from his throat!

There came a sudden exclamation from within. A rustling sound. Then silence. Masters groaned again. He thumped on the wall, lurched, groaned a third time, and pounded once on the locked door.

"Doctor! Oh, doctor!" he cried in a weak voice.

A snarled curse was the answer, then the rasp of a key in the lock. The unkempt head of the hunchback appeared against the hellish green incandescence of the room.

Mouthing thick, inarticulate sounds, Masters lurched forward into the room, despite a half-hearted attempt to stay him on the threshold. The detective was bent over, gripping his stomach now with one hand. His face was contorted with seeming agony. Such was his real horror of this thing he had uncovered, that he actually felt a nausea which drove the blood from his cheeks, and opened his pores to chill perspiration.

"I... ate apple... poisoned..." he gasped. "Can't you— give me... something... stop pain...."

Then he half fell into a chair, atop a pile of books, breaking away from the vise grip which the chemist had fastened on his arm. "Oh, help me, doctor!" he implored, voice rising to a scream. "I... that poison... can't you do *some*thing?"

The hunchbacked body of the chemist was trembling. Passion and fright distorted his features. His gnarled arms reached out as though to clutch the unwelcome visitor and throw him out of the apartment. But he checked himself.

"Dammit! Why did you come back here?" he snarled. "What is wrong? Pain, you say? The apple? Impossible. Dose apples...."

He looked up at the half-window of the room, one which opened to the courtyard in the rear. Then he seemed to reach a decision.

"Of course I wish to help. You maybe should go to a hospital? Or is it really serious? You really have terrible pains?" With shaking fingers he sloshed some gin into a glass, and held it to Jigger's lips. "Here, drink this. It cannot be the poison. You would be dead long ago. But pains! I—I cannot understand it at all! Tell me what happened."

Amid groans he sought to make realistically horrible, the detective told in a few snatches of words how he had walked to the subway station at Seventy-second, munching his apple. How suddenly these terrible cramps had come on, just as he was about to board a train. How he suspected it might be some more of the same poison which had done for Crosetti, Nahigian and Julie LeGendre....

Convulsions seemed to clutch him, and he gulped some more of the liquor. Dr. Tork let go of him, and paced swayingly up and down the room.

An idea seemed to strike him. Paying no more attention to Masters, he walked into the chamber adjoining, took out his upper plate of false teeth, and was busy for a moment with one of the big inlays set for camouflage—or possibly ornament—in one of the twelve-year molars. In the other room Masters continued to groan, though not loudly enough to bring others from the upstairs apartments. He did not dare attempt to watch what was happening. He hated this role of Judas; yet this man had named himself the wickedest man in New York. He deserved no consideration.

REPLACING THE PLATE of false teeth in his upper jaw, Dr. Tork then took a hypodermic needle from its case in a small drawer, and placed it carefully in the pocket of a jacket hanging there. Then he donned the jacket over his grimy shirt, and strode back to his supposedly dying patient.

"You haf need of a stomach poomp, if this is really poison, my friend!" he announced breathlessly. "I haf not it here. I can do nothing. But there is a hospital a few blocks over—Central Park West. I shall take you there. It would not do... if you were to die here..." The last words were a mutter.

No, Masters supposed grimly that another corpse in this basement apartment might be rather hard to explain. Much better for Tork to cart him somewhere outdoors, then finish him off if he were not already dead, and leave him in some dark areaway for the police to find.

"I—can't walk!" groaned Masters, bent double.

"Come, come, I haf a little car. It will be only up the steps and out. I will bring the little car," said Tork cajolingly. "Then at the hospital—"

The detective straightened. Gone from his countenance now was all the contortion of feigned agony.

"Oh, you have a car, have you?" he asked coldly. "A Chevrolet, no doubt? Isn't that a good guess, Doctor Tork?"

In his right hand now was a police whistle. He raised it to his lips. The whistle shrilled.

Comprehension, fear and rage leapt instantly to the seamed face of the chemist.

"You... *knew!*" he screeched, fumbling in his jacket pocket for the hypodermic, getting hold of it, yanking it loose from the lining of the pocket as he jumped at Jigger Masters.

The latter flashed out his automatic with a swift gesture, stepping back as he saw he had only a split second of time. One shot crashed.

The silvery hypodermic needle vanished from Tork's hand as if by legerdemain. The top part of a blunt, dirty thumb, which had been on the plunger, vanished with it. A throaty scream of different timbre burst from the hunched killer. He flung himself forward, grappling with Masters, preventing him from firing a second aimed shot.

For three or four long seconds then the detective tasted the full, superman strength of maniacal fury. Himself an athlete in good trim, Masters had always been amusedly tolerant of these tales in which a madman will overcome two or even three men normally stronger than himself. But now he knew how true it was. Tork gripped him, paralyzed those sinewy arms, flung him backward toward an ancient chair.

Masters felt the arm of the chair behind his thighs. He was bending backward… back….

The killer, making exultant, horrible noises in his throat, suddenly shifted his grip, bloody hand and all, going for the detective's throat.

Then an avalanche of blue-coated police burst through the locked door, pausing not, but launching themselves… one… two… three… four of them, straight at Dr. Ivan Tork. And even then a nightstick had to rise and fall twice, before the mêlée of arms, legs and torsos quieted down.

"So… he's the wickedest man!" panted Captain Haight, who had provided the handcuffs. "What a—a monster!"

"Quite!" agreed Masters grimly. "If all my cases were of this sort, I'd get me a nice, sweet job in the street-cleaning department. But you can't pick and choose; crime is always a filthy business." He turned to the prisoner.

"You must realize, doctor," he said, "that the evidence of the apple, the hypodermic, and the Chevrolet of which Julie spoke, will be unbeatable against you. Do you want to tell us why you murdered those three people?"

A snarl came in answer. "What do I care for evidence? I succeeded. Death is nothing. I only wish you had really eaten that apple, my smart young friend! For a time you puzzled me, for my poison works as well in the stomach as in the arteries, though not as quickly."

"What is the poison?" put in Haight. "Something new?"

"Yah-h, it is new. Go to hell!" snarled Tork. "You will neffer find out!"

AND THAT WAS true enough. They never discovered the

exact compound which Tork had used, though its nature, as a complex molecule in which cyanogen (C_2N_2) had its action speeded by some catalytic substance, was guessed at rather closely.

Masters and the police, working together, did uncover the reason why Dr. Ivan Tork hated Frank Crosetti and Julie LeGendre. The killing of the *cigo*-maker, Nahigian, had been merely incidental; to keep him from telling how Tork had visited the place, and seen a shipment of *cigos* already boxed, and ready to go to Frank Crosetti.

The original hatred against Crosetti and Julie had its foundation in one of the oldest of all human motives—jealousy.

"It's terrible, and somehow I feel we don't quite understand all of it yet," said Masters to Captain Haight. "The truth is that for some odd reason, Julie LeGendre, as a young girl, married Ivan Tork! She divorced him in Reno, when Frank Crosetti came on the scene. Dr. Tork never forgave either of them.

"The queer part comes in how Tork ever got hold of her in the first place."

"Oh, women are nuts," shrugged Captain Haight.

In his cell in the Tombs, awaiting trial, Dr. Ivan Tork finished the third and last page of his confession, and signed his crabbed name. This fearful document, which even the tabloids would not publish in full, was the record of a brilliant mind congenitally unhinged. The offspring of a marriage of cousins, one of whom had been tubercular, Ivan Tork had been twisted in brain as well as in body, from birth.

One paragraph of that awesome record, deleted of its gloating, is worth reproducing.

> Her father had been my friend, and made me the legal guardian of his beautiful girl-child. I controlled her modest fortune, but soon lost it in speculation, during the panic of 1907. From that time on, impelled as much by fear of discovery as by the supreme physical lure of Julie, I forced her little by little to accept me as her husband-to-be. When she was sixteen, I married her. Then nothing could be done to me. Of course she was always a strange girl, and hated me, though she never learned about the money....

Putting down his pen, Dr. Tork glared about his cell. In the corridor a guard paced up and down. The scientist reached in and drew forth the upper plate of his false teeth. Unscrewing the ornamental inlay in one twelve-year molar, he plucked forth a tiny ampoule of poison. Thrusting this back on his tongue, he swallowed.

Thirty seconds later the guard found him writhing in convulsions. A minute later he was stone dead.

Masters read the confession an hour later. He put it down and his face was pale.

"So it was treachery, embezzlement—and lust!" he said sternly. "After that, I think we can forgive Julie LeGendre almost anything she did against men! And I am inclined to believe, Haight, that Dr. Ivan Tork merited in full the title he gave himself, the wickedest man in the world!"

www.ingramcontent.com/pod-product-compliance
Lightning Source LLC
Chambersburg PA
CBHW030545030726
47495CB00004B/1144